Starstruck

OBSESSED

BETH CIOTTA

BC Ink

ALSO BY BETH CIOTTA

Impossible Dream

BEAUTY & THE BIKER
ENCHANTING CHRISTMAS

The Cupcake Lovers

FOOL FOR LOVE
THE TROUBLE WITH LOVE
ANYTHING BUT LOVE
SOME KIND OF WONDERFUL
IN THE MOOD FOR LOVE

Peacemakers (Old West)
LASSO THE MOON
ROMANCING THE WEST
FALL OF ROME

The Glorious Victorious Darcys
HER SKY COWBOY
HIS BROKEN ANGEL
HIS CLOCKWORK CANARY

For an extensive booklist, visit Beth's website
www.bethciotta.com

PRAISE FOR BETH CIOTTA'S NOVELS

"Charming, witty and magical. A Must-Read!"—*Tasty Read Book Reviews* (on *Beauty & the Biker*)

"Filled with humor, heart and touch of mystery, this is a truly magical book." –*Born to Read Books* (on *Beauty & the Biker*)

"Deep love of family and strong dialogue bolster a refreshing romance that focuses on the emotional rather than the physical." –*Publishers Weekly* (on *In the Mood for Love*)

"Ciotta writes fun, sexy reads with a good dose of realism." — *RT BOOKreviews* (on *The Trouble With Love*)

"Ciotta's wit adds spark to this tale of extended-family joys and sorrows, smalltown living, and complicated characters." –*Publishers Weekly* (on *Fool for Love*)

"Enchanting contemporary romance." –*Publishers Weekly* (on *Charmed*)

"Ciotta has written another imaginative, whirlwind adventure, featuring a daring hero and a spirited heroine, incredible inventions, and übernefarious villains." –*Booklist*, starred review (on *His Clockwork Canary*)

ABOUT THE SERIES

Welcome to STARSTRUCK, a showplace for talent, a playground for love. A contemporary continuity series by Beth Ciotta, Cynthia Valero, and Elle J Rossi. Three authors. One world.

Indulge and enjoy!

***

(novellas sold separately)

OBSESSED by Beth Ciotta
WRECKED by Cynthia Valero
JADED by Elle J Rossi

***

BETH CIOTTA

One

"I need you, Mac."

He'd waited seven years to hear those words.

Wyatt MacDermott eased away from the woman sleeping in his bed to focus on the woman who'd been his first and last celebrity client. Rusty Ann Baker. An award-winning, chart-busting singing sensation who'd since retired from the business. A woman who'd won and refused his affections. Their friendship, however, was solid and Wyatt was forever in her debt.

Pulling on his shorts, he moved onto the balcony of his fifth-story condo, greeting the sunrise with a dull headache and accelerated pulse. "When and where?"

"Soonest and Starstruck."

The Midwestern night club she owned and ran along with her new husband. Although they'd been married, hell, two years now. Not so new. "I'll take the first flight out."

Straight run from the Jersey Shore to Philly, direct flight to O'Hare, hour drive to Kramer—a landlocked town on the

1

fringes of Chicago. He'd be there before nightfall.

"I'm not interrupting an assignment, am I?"

"No."

"In between gigs then."

"Something like that." His director, Ian Briggs of Briggs Operations and Security Specialists, aka B.O.S.S., had ordered Wyatt to take some downtime. "*Get a life*," he'd said. What he meant was: *Get some therapy.*

She blew out a breath. "Great. Because I'm not sure how long I'll need you."

"I'm in for the haul."

"Before you commit, you should know the specifics. I know you said, anytime, anywhere, any reason, but—"

"No buts. I'm there."

"Mac."

"Fine. If it'll make you feel better, spill." Wyatt glanced over his shoulder, through the partially opened sliding glass door. He wasn't hiding this conversation from Suzanne, just affording her a chance to sleep in.

Chance blown she told him with a smile and a cocky wave as she rolled out of bed and into his bathroom.

Friends more than lovers, Wyatt welcomed her casual acceptance of his barely-dawn desertion.

"Dakota Breeze," Rusty said.

Any warmth Wyatt had felt at the sound of Rusty's voice froze over at the mention of the tarnished celebrity's name. A hot-mess of controversy and scandal, Dakota Breeze pushed a lot of people's buttons. Including Wyatt's.

"I know you have issues, but she's a good kid, Mac."

A matter of opinion and not one Wyatt shared. "She's not a kid anymore," he said, skirting deeper thoughts. "She's what? Thirty? Thirty-one?"

"And still finding her way. Like a lot of other people her age," Rusty pressed on. "Anyway, we have a history. Sort of like you and me. May-December. Younger-older—"

"Got it." The fact that Rusty was sixteen years Wyatt's senior had never been an issue for him, but damn she'd been conventional on that front. "You're fond of Dakota which—given the age difference—puts you in mother mode."

"Don't be a prick."

"What do you need, Rusty?" Wyatt focused on the serene

waves of the Atlantic as the woman he'd once protected with his life waged her defense for a spoiled pop singer who'd tripped into fame and fortune at age fourteen and, five years later—after a headline grabbing scandal—plunged head first into tabloid torture. A laughing stock before age twenty. A has-been at twenty-one. Dakota Breeze had fumbled through the past ten years with a string of failed projects and broken engagements. Not that Wyatt followed that gossip, but his little sister did. Plus, Dakota's escapades had been on display at most checkout counters up until she'd faded into relative obscurity.

"Dakota's people are pushing for a comeback."

"Her people."

"She says she wants it, too, but I think that's lip service. She's spent her entire life trying to please and impress everyone in her circle, not to mention her fans. This isn't about resurrecting her passion. It's about feeding a habit. I sensed it when we spoke on the phone. Now that she's here…"

Rusty trailed off and Wyatt breathed deep. The tang of salt and sea teased his nostrils, but all he smelled was trouble.

"I offered Starstruck as a safe place for Dakota to rehearse her new show. I thought I was doing her a favor, sheltering her from the paparazzi. Who would look for her in Kramer, Illinois? As long as she kept her head in her work and out of the spotlight."

"I'm guessing that didn't last long."

"I blame her entourage. And since Dakota's bodyguard is a wannabe action star, he tends to attract attention instead of keeping it at bay. I've spent the past two days shadowing my friend, fending off curious fans and trying to talk sense into her crafty manager. The man flaunts Dakota's name everywhere they go. How long before the paparazzi shows up? I don't have the time or patience to deal with the drama and I'm not keen on burdening my small security crew with keeping Dakota shielded and safe. They've got their hands full with monitoring the nightly crowds at Starstruck."

The thought of Rusty going toe-to-toe with trouble of any sort chafed Wyatt's ass. "Where's Frank?" He'd never met Rusty's second husband, but he knew from things she'd said that Frank Janus, a top-notch sound tech, was a loving and protective husband—unlike the first asshole she'd said "yes" to.

"Frank's on tour, filling in for an old friend. He wanted to come home, but I talked him out of it. Abandoning the audio crew and band on little to no notice isn't his style. And it's not like my situation is dire. Still, he said he'd feel better if I had additional backup. Since you're a professional and someone I already trust, he suggested you."

Wyatt raised a brow. "How does he even know about me?"

"You saved my life, Mac. Of course, I told him about you."

"Does he know I had a thing for you?" Actually, Wyatt still had a thing for Rusty, but that was his problem, not hers.

"Back in the day, a lot of men had a thing for me."

He could mention timeless beauty, but that would only make her uncomfortable. Even without seeing Rusty, Wyatt knew, at fifty-two, she still turned heads.

"Frank's not the jealous sort."

"Uh-huh."

"Okay. Let's say I don't give him any reason to be jealous."

"That I believe." Wyatt moved back into his bedroom, nabbing Suzanne's hand and giving it a squeeze before she made her exit. Alone now he moved to his laptop, anxious to book a flight. Anxious to race to Rusty's rescue. "So you want me to keep the paparazzi and fans in line so you and your team can focus on business as usual."

"I want you to afford Dakota the privacy she needs to get her shit together."

Wyatt punched "book" even as his own reservations rose. As far as he was concerned, Dakota was a self-absorbed train wreck. Her obsession with fame consistently warped her judgment. As a result, she was a proven danger to herself as well as others.

"I want you to protect her from anyone who stresses her out and that includes her entourage. She buckles under pressure. You don't."

A woman Wyatt respected, a woman he'd loved, was asking him to coddle someone he resented. "You're asking me to hold her hand."

"You held mine."

"On the rare occasion you let me. Not to mention you were in physical danger at the time."

"Yeah, well, that's another thing, Mac. Dakota may be at risk."

"How so?"

"You know she got some death threats after that concert catastrophe that sparked her famous breakdown, right?"

He shifted, uncomfortable with this discussion, but determined to see it through. "That was twelve years ago."

"Yeah, but I'm worried news leaked about this comeback and irritated an old wound. I found a letter yesterday. Mixed in with my business mail but addressed to Dakota. I was with her when she opened it. That's the only reason I'm privy to the content."

"And?"

"It was ugly, Mac. A vile worded note basically telling her to retire for good...or else. I wanted to call the police, but Dakota swore me to silence. She said it's not the first time she's gotten hate mail, and yes, it's upsetting, but she's learned to shrug it off like a bad review. She's convinced acknowledgment of any sort only fans the flames. I agree to a certain extent, but what if she's wrong in this instance? What if ignoring the threat is the exact wrong thing to do? At the very least she should alert her team to potential trouble so they can be on the lookout for any suspicious activity, right?"

"That would be a sensible precaution, yes."

"Except Dakota's convinced the threat is benign. As such, she doesn't want to needlessly worry or distract anyone from this brutal preliminary rehearsal. End result, no one in her entourage, including that preening excuse for a bodyguard, knows about the letter."

"But you're breaking your promise and telling me."

"I told Dakota the only way I'd keep the news to myself was if she allowed me to bring in a specialist of my own choice. I told her as long as she's under my roof she has to abide by my rules."

Spoken like a confident, caring, and doting mother.

Wyatt kept that thought to himself. He was too busy packing to get into an argument with Rusty. She'd never admit it, but she looked after everyone in her circle with the rabid devotion of a she-wolf, utilizing the same kindness she'd showered on her only son, often setting aside her own needs in deference to others. She gave everyone the benefit of the doubt, even when the rest of the world pegged someone as a bitch or a bastard. It's what had landed her in a fix with her asshole first husband. Now she was potentially in harm's way because of Dakota Breeze.

"Since we're having this discussion," Wyatt said as he moved into the bathroom to shower, "I assume Ms. Breeze agreed to my protection."

"She agreed."

"But she isn't happy about it."

"No, she is not. So, if she's not very nice to you—"

"I'll live."

As much as Wyatt dreaded this job, he didn't want Rusty to regret reaching out. Although she knew he had a problem with irresponsible celebrities, she wasn't aware he had a personal beef with Dakota. This, he told himself, was merely a twisted quirk of fate and nothing he couldn't handle. He'd take a bullet for Rusty. Granting this favor wouldn't be nearly as painful. At worst, Dakota was salt in an ancient wound and, truth told, Wyatt had a sudden and morbid compulsion to put a crimp in her reckless lifestyle.

"Out of curiosity," he said, "considering Dakota already has a bodyguard, how are you explaining my presence to her manager?"

"I told Van Mitchell that I didn't trust his chosen muscle any farther then I could throw him. Starstruck is my club and Dakota is my friend. I don't want any trouble for either. And as long as they're rehearsing on my stage—"

"Your house, your rules." Wyatt smiled a little, remembering what Rusty was like when riled. "So this Mitchell character knows I answer to you, not him."

"He knows." She blew out a breath. "You're a doll to this, Mac. And Dakota... She really is a good kid."

An unspoken *just like you* hung in the air as Rusty unintentionally kicked Wyatt's heart with her undying gratitude.

Two

Kramer, IL
Saturday, June 13, the midnight reckoning

Wyatt had had his share of disastrous travel days, but today took the cake. Delayed flight, missed connection, botched rental service. By the time he rolled into Kramer, Illinois, it was nearly midnight and his mood was as black as the suburban sky.

He'd been in communication with Rusty throughout the day. "*Not to worry,*" she'd said more than once. "*I've got Dakota's back.*" Which only ramped up his unease. That meant Rusty was in harm's way if Dakota was in genuine danger. The wannabe action star bodyguard was as unreliable as Rusty feared. Wyatt's research indicated Dakota's handlers had plucked Pauley Bright out of a gym, not a legit agency or program. All show, no training.

On the other hand, her road manager had a decent track record and her choreographer had won a couple of music video awards. The long day had given Wyatt more than enough time to bone up on the full cast—a mixed bag of seasoned professionals and hungry newbies. Because she was supposed to be honing her new act in secret, Dakota was operating with a minimal crew. According to Rusty, the dethroned pop queen was rehearsing to pre-recorded tracks, so no musicians were in the mix. She'd trimmed her crew to just six dancers, a choreographer, a PA, a chauffeur, a nutritionist/trainer, a bodyguard, and her road manager. *Just.*

After researching every name on the list and discussing personalities and duties with Rusty, Wyatt mentally dismissed at least four out of the twelve yahoos. The more people in Dakota's immediate circle the greater the chance of screw ups and leaks. A discussion he'd have with his new principal first thing in the morning.

His immediate goal was to get inside Starstruck. The sooner he stepped in as Dakota's bodyguard, the sooner Rusty could step away. Far away if Wyatt had anything to say about it.

He spied his former client's pride and joy a quarter mile out. Aside from a gas station and an all-night café, Kramer—advertised as a small town with big city amenities—had shut down for the night. The largest entertainment complex in Grundy County was well marked with a blinding neon sign. The bright blue and shocking pink letters flashed STARSTRUCK but screamed *good times*. More modest and intriguing than any of the marquees illuminating the casinos in Wyatt's neck of the woods, yet equally effective.

The parking lot was packed.

He pulled his rented wheels in between two pickup trucks then surveyed the surroundings while making his way to the front door. Starstruck, a combination dance club and concert hall, rivaled a number of popular themed venues around the country in size and atmosphere. The rock foundation and rustic beams promoted a good ol' boy vibe. Or maybe that was the shit-kicking music pulsing through the humid summer air. Music that reminded him of his days on the road with Rusty.

The frustrations of the day fell away as Wyatt shifted into protector mode. Highly trained, fiercely devoted, he lapsed into the mindset that simultaneously impressed and concerned his boss. Emotions in ironclad check. Even his affection for Rusty and his grievances with Dakota were in lock down. What Wyatt considered a hard won skill, Ian called a crutch.

Wyatt pushed that conversation out of his mind, focusing on the present sights and sounds. Acclimating to the chaos.

Although there wasn't a line of people waiting to get in, the entrance was clogged with clubbers desperate for a smoke or a dose of fresh air. Dudes in jeans and t-shirts. Chicks in a wide range of fashion, all of it tight.

Overdressed in a casual suit and open-necked oxford, Wyatt shouldered his way through the sweaty mix of patrons and came face-to-thick-neck with a mountain of a man.

"No wristband. No entrance," thick-neck said.

"Ten dollar cover charge," came a higher pitched voice.

Wyatt smiled at the young woman sitting at a podium next to thick-neck. They were both dressed in black jeans and snug black tees bearing the blue and pink logo of Starstruck. "Wyatt MacDermott to see Rusty Ann Baker."

Thick-neck shifted closer. "ID?"

Wyatt flashed his credentials while noting the badge dangling off of a blue lanyard imprinted with pink guitars. Charlie. Security. Charlie was sharp and willing to wear pink. Two points for Charlie.

"Boss lady's expecting you," he said, his deep voice somehow cutting through a screaming loud guitar solo. "Follow me."

Wyatt complied. He also scoped out the club's main room. Two bars—one at the east end, one along the northern wall. The stage—tricked out with high tech audio and lighting—dominated the west end. He noted the designated exits, doors leading to other rooms, a spiral stairway leading to the second floor, and the crowded tables and the jammed dance floor. The music was deafening, but good. Not that he expected anything less. Rusty booked the talent and her expectations regarding music and performing had always been high.

Charlie unclasped the chain blocking the entrance to the spiral staircase. He motioned Wyatt ahead of him. "Top of the stairs, take a left. Rusty's on Star Deck, the private party room, along with the diva and her crew. Good luck man. Better you than me."

Wyatt scaled the steps. He glanced to the right, noting a private office—Rusty's office. Per his request, she'd emailed a scanned blueprint allowing him to memorize the club's layout ahead of time. Second floor—private offices to the right, private party space to the left.

Star Deck—a balcony with a prime view of the action—also included an alcove featuring a premium stocked bar, additional speakers, low lighting, and plush seating.

Wyatt studied the partying occupants from the shadows, matching faces with names based on Rusty's descriptions. A group of pretty, skinny people were cutting loose on a small dance floor. A bulked-up pretty-boy—Pauley-the-rent-a-bodyguard—was making time with the pretty, young bartender.

Dakota Breeze, the prettiest of them all, sat at the other end of the bar, her long, satiny legs crossed, her fingers drumming impatiently on a tall glass of something as a fair-haired man yakked in her ear. Wyatt pegged blond-boy as her road manager, Van Mitchell, who'd been appointed by Dakota's longtime career manager, Roger Smith, a mentor who'd taken over the reins from her first manager—who also happened to be her father.

The woman was a walking cliché.

She was also stunning, in an overtly sexual way. Gorgeous face, generous curves—unlike her dancing, lanky friends—thick, tousled golden-brown hair that fell to the small of her back.

Her most powerful asset, however, was charisma. That enigmatic magic packed a powerful punch—even at a distance. Easy to see how Dakota had mesmerized his sister and an entire generation of teens.

Wyatt assessed the troubled performer with detached fascination.

"She's somethin', huh?"

He didn't answer, but he did smile down at the woman who'd moved in beside him. Five-foot-six of genuine star power. Faded jeans, flowery blouse, turquoise cowboy boots. Big blue eyes and cherry red hair. Ageless crossed his mind, along with sexy.

"Glad you made it okay," Rusty said. She matched his smile. "Good to see you, Mac. I'd hug you, but I can see you're in work mode. Wouldn't want to squash that badass vibe."

"I think I can maintain badass while greeting a friend." Wyatt welcomed a quick squeeze from the woman who'd once likened his affection to a talent crush. "Beautiful as ever. Frank's a lucky man."

"Except for the times I'm a pain in the ass," she said with a teasing smile before turning serious. "Frank appreciates you being here, Mac. And I can't thank you enough. I think the world of Dakota."

"Even though she's a diva."

"That's an act. When you get to know her better, you'll see through it, too."

Just then, Dakota looked their way. She slid off the stool, her short dress hitching just shy of her crotch. Jesus. Her long legs eating up the distance between them, her stride impressively steady given those five-inch stilettos. At least she wasn't drunk.

"You must be Mac."

And you're the woman who rained misery on my family.

He waited for anger to well.

Instead, confusion banged at his practiced indifference as he experienced Dakota Breeze up close and in person.

Plumped glossy lips. Perfect bleached teeth. Thick false lashes. Was her long hair extensions? Her full breasts implants?

She was something all right.

If you went for cosmetically enhanced, self-absorbed screw-ups.

At the same time he sensed something else. Something that grabbed him by the nads and challenged his expectations. He noted then dismissed the sensation, reminding himself this woman was a player.

She did her own quick assessment of Wyatt, hiking her chin and narrowing her kohl-lined, laser-green eyes. "What the hell took you so long?"

She tossed a look over her shoulder, called to her dancing minions. "Go down and have fun, Darlings. I'm out of here. Pauley, you stay and keep them out of trouble. Van—"

"I'm coming with you." Mitchell had been on screaming red heels and now he gave Wyatt the stink eye.

"We don't know you, MacDermott."

"No, but I do," Rusty said.

"If he's good enough for Rusty, he's good enough for me," Dakota said as if Wyatt wasn't standing right there. "We talked about this, Van. Now get off my ass. I can't breathe. Stay here. Have fun. I'm going back to my room to get some R&R. Let's go," she said to Wyatt then air-kissed Rusty and sauntered toward the stairs.

If the diva thing was an act, she had it down pat.

Rusty raised her brows at Wyatt, offering a smile that said both "Sorry" and "Good luck".

Mitchell grabbed his arm. "If you let anything happen..." He trailed off reading the warning in Wyatt's eyes and loosening his hold. He worked his jaw. "Yeah, well, I'll be checking in."

"You do that," Wyatt said while catching up to Dakota. He finessed his way in front of her, taking the lead as they went down the stairs. The club was dark with the exception of a retro mirror ball and assorted laser lights. Most eyes were fixed on the wailing band, a dancing partner, or drinking buddy. If Wyatt ushered Dakota through the thick of the crowd some of those eyes would turn to her. Not wanting the attention, any attention, he hooked her waist as they hit the floor and swung her toward the closest door. Down the hall, through another door, into the kitchen...

"The rear exit escape," she said as he whisked her past two wide-eyed fry cooks. "How dramatic."

No drama at all.

Exactly how he wanted it.

Out the door, past the loading dock, down four steps onto a concrete lot. He'd memorized the interior and exterior layout. Maybe this was overkill, but better safe than sorry. Even if she wasn't famous she could start a small riot in that tiny, skin-tight dress and killer heels.

"Slow down for chrissake."

"I could carry you."

"Or you could slow down."

Scoping the perimeter for lurking photographers or suspicious characters, Wyatt kept the pace, tightening his hold as he whisked her through the shadows and into his car. All the while, aware of his surroundings. Aware of her scent.

Aware of her luscious curves tucked tight against his hard body.

"Enjoy that, did you?" she asked with a smirk, shoving aside his hand when he tried to buckle her into the passenger seat.

More than he should have. More than he'd braced for. He should have locked down his libido along with his emotions. His untimely arousal was a damned brain buster. He harbored a longtime grudge tied to the detrimental influence she'd had on his sister. Dakota wasn't directly to blame for the incident that had altered Kerry's life, still... Yeah. There was that. Plus, she wasn't his type. Not in looks. Not in temperament. He'd never been a fan of her music so he couldn't even attribute the unexpected boner to a shallow talent crush.

What the hell?

He keyed the address of the country estate she was renting into his GPS.

"Uh, uh," Dakota said. "Not yet. There's an all-night café back toward town. I'm starving."

So much for calling it a night. So much for low-profile. In a brightly lit café, she'd be the focus of every red-blooded man and green-eyed woman. He raked his gaze over her body then raised a brow telegraphing his thoughts regarding her attention grabbing attire.

"Don't worry about it," she snapped as he put the car in gear. Dragging her tousled hair off her face, she whipped it into a messy half-knot/half ponytail then dug in her designer purse and shoved on a pair of blue-tinted glasses.

"Nice disguise."

"He speaks!"

Wyatt deflected her sarcasm by focusing on the road. She probably ate like a bird. With any luck they'd be in and out of the café in twenty minutes.

Twenty minutes of hell.

He'd curse Rusty if he weren't so fond of her. If he didn't owe her. If he didn't...

"You don't talk much, do you, Mac?"

"Only when I have something to say."

Three

What a nightmare.

Dakota hadn't been thrilled about Rusty's insistence on bringing another bodyguard on board, but now that Wyatt MacDermott was actually here she was downright depressed. At least Pauley, as irritating as he was, was jovial. Mac, as Rusty called him, had a stick up his ass.

Big time.

The strong, conventional, unbendable, silent type. Rusty had described him as a top-notch professional with a solid gold heart. More like a heart of stone, Dakota thought as she rooted in her uber big bag of tricks. She hadn't detected an iota of warmth in his icy grey gaze. Just judgmental condemnation. He didn't like her. She didn't care.

Okay. That was a lie. She cared. That, more than anything, soured her already cranky mood. She'd assured her therapist she no longer viewed her worth through the eyes of others. In truth, it was a work in progress.

As soon as Ice Man focused on the road, Dakota toed off her spikey heels and shimmied into the pair of baggy black lounging pants she'd had balled in her purse. Cloaked in darkness, she peeled her metallic dress over her head and yanked on a shapeless tee. If her new bodyguard snuck a peek at her lacey black bra, she didn't notice. Accustomed to quick changes, the entire transformation took less than ten seconds and that included pulling on a pair of non-descript ballet flats.

Nice disguise.

His sarcasm rang in her ears and stoked her temper. Did he honestly think she assumed she could obscure her identity by slapping on a pair of shades? Did he think she was a complete hack in the art of laying low?

The only reason she'd decked out in clubbing clothes was to blend with the partying crowd. If she'd gone overboard it was because she typically frequented techno dance clubs, not urban cowboy mega-bars. Not that she'd been up for a night of partying in the first place, but her dancers (Dakota's Darlings) had begged her to join them. They'd worked their butts off all week. Denying them hadn't been an option. Rusty had been the one to talk them into hanging at Starstruck instead of driving into Chicago, promising a private room and an open bar. Dakota had hoped to skip out after an hour, but then Mac had been delayed and since she'd made that deal with Rusty, she'd had to wait for him to arrive.

Unwilling to focus on why they'd struck that deal, Dakota focused on the result.

Wyatt MacDermott was younger than she'd expected. Mid-thirties maybe? She'd assumed he'd be closer in age to Rusty, considering they were friends. Although she was tight with Rusty, too, so that was a stupid assumption now that she thought about it. Maybe it was the way Rusty talked about him—so respectful and admiring—that intimated he was older.

Thinking back, Rusty had focused solely on his professional background. She hadn't said anything about him being insanely gorgeous. Surely she'd noticed. Any breathing woman would. Not that Dakota was attracted.

Another lie. And it pissed her off because she had a history of being attracted to men who, eventually, treated her like shit. Mac was ahead of the game on that front. His obvious disapproval and cold indifference was outright rude. Although he *was* pulling into the lot of Blackbirds Country

Café instead of the driveway of her rented house. Indulging her whim instead of hiding her away, which was what she knew Rusty—God love her caring soul—would have preferred. Maybe that stick was only halfway up his ass.

"Here's the thing," Dakota said as Mac tucked away his keys and released his seat belt. "You can't tell anyone we came here. Meaning anyone in my entourage. Especially Van. No, especially Terrance. My personal trainer. He wouldn't approve and I don't want to hear it, so... don't say anything. Although, I guess that's not something I have to worry about," she added in the wake of his silent stare.

Huffing a breath, she nabbed her purse and pushed open her door, stunned to see him standing in front of her when she emerged from the sporty four-door. Silent like the wind in more ways than one.

Now that she was wearing flats, Mac towered above her. He was also overdressed compared to her. "If you don't want to attract attention," she said, "take off your jacket. People are more casual around here."

"Don't worry about it," he said, repeating her words and ignoring her suggestion. He briefly palmed the small of her back, prompting her toward the café.

Dakota ignored her tingling spine. The same tingle that had rippled through her body with the subtlety of a tidal wave when he'd pulled her into his side, whisking her away from Starstruck.

It didn't help that she'd been celibate for more than a year. It didn't help that she was rattled by a myriad of doubts and fears and here he was—a big, bad protection specialist who typically shielded politicians and dignitaries. Which put him in a league apart from Pauley and the typical celebrity muscle as far as Dakota was concerned. Instead of swatting away pesky paparazzi, Mac protected VIPs from dangerous assassins and she was in serious awe.

Hero worship.

She was used to being on the receiving end. Not the other way around.

Her infatuation was text-book pathetic. But at least she recognized it for what it was. At least she could put this earthshaking attraction to the man in perspective. Which gave her a modicum of self-control. Something she'd lacked in the past.

Now if she could only exhibit that kind of restraint when she ordered off the menu.

Two minutes later they were seated opposite of each other in a booth. Dakota slumped in her seat and buried her face in the multi-page menu. Part of this comeback concert entailed wearing skimpy costumes, something she was famous for, and performing complicated dance routines, something she was also famous for. Except she wasn't fifteen anymore. She was thirty-one and thirty pounds over her famous one-hundred-and-three-pounds-soaking-wet weight. Although due to severe food maintenance and brutal exercise, she was slowly edging toward her former physique. Binging and sabotaging all that hard work was stupid. She could hear Van in one ear and Terrance in the other telling her so.

"Screw it. I'll have two fried eggs over easy," Dakota said when the waitress showed to take their order. "A heap of bacon, rye toast *with* butter, and a side of pancakes. Oh, and a strawberry milkshake."

Setting aside the menu, Dakota glanced at Mac, braced for censure or at least a facial tick that betrayed surprise or amusement. At the very least, she expected him to order something disgustingly healthy or nothing at all.

He surprised her on all counts.

"I'll have the same," he told the waitress. "Although make my shake chocolate. Extra thick. Thanks."

The waitress left with their menus and Dakota narrowed her eyes on the man who'd yet to crack a smile, raise a brow, or to display any expression whatsoever. "How do you do that?" she asked. "That freaky poker face thing."

"It's a skill."

"Why did you order what I ordered?"

"Sounded good."

"It's fattening, you know."

"I can take it."

"I was talking about myself."

"Is this where I'm supposed to tell you that you don't need to worry about your figure? That you're beautiful the way you are?"

Dakota flushed. She didn't mistake his response for a compliment. He wasn't flirting. He was judging. Again. She was so freaking tired of everyone judging her every move, every word. She was sick of the assumptions and conjectures, sick of being monitored and manipulated. Even Rusty, the most accepting and genuine person in her small circle of friends, had talked her into something she didn't want.

Wyatt MacDermott.

"Kiss my ass." She grabbed her purse and set to leave.

Mac stilled her with a barely-there touch of his hand. "Sorry."

The unexpected apology took the heat out of her bluster.

"You're hungry. I'm hungry," he said. "Let's eat."

On cue, the waitress moved in with a tray loaded with greasy, buttery to-die-for fried food.

Dakota settled in her seat even though her nerves were still on edge. She waited until their plates and drinks were served, until the waitress faded away. Waited until she tasted her first delectable mouthful of crispy bacon followed by a forkful of pancakes soaked in maple syrup. Waited until they'd almost finished their meals before she attempted civilized (or otherwise) conversation. Mostly she tried not to watch Mac eat because for some reason watching this man chow down was a massive turn-on.

Did he eat like that all the time? Did he work out obsessively? Was he one of those people who could devour anything and never gain an ounce? How did he stay so trim? Was he ripped under that dark suit? Of course, he was ripped. Or at the very least, in prime condition. He wouldn't get winded during one dance routine. His muscles wouldn't cramp after a five-mile run. Stamina probably ranked high on his list of skills alongside indifference.

"I'm on a strict diet and training regimen," she blurted. "That's why I don't want you tell my people about this side trip. Everyone's working so hard to ensure the success of this show."

"According to Rusty, no one's working harder than you."

Dakota blinked.

"Said that choreographer's putting you through your paces. Called him a sadist. Said the same thing about your personal trainer."

She cursed Brock and Terrence every day, along with Van. Still, she felt compelled to defend them. "They're just doing their jobs."

"So am I." He pulled out his wallet. "Let's go."

"What?" His abruptness caught her off guard. Did he sense trouble? She glanced over her shoulder. Yes, it was crowded, but no one was coming their way. No photographer. No pen-wielding fan begging for an autograph. No pissed off parent accusing her of poisoning their young kid's mind. "I haven't finished my shake," she said, which sounded lame but this was the first semi-normal moment she'd had all week.

"We'll get it to go." He motioned for the waitress.

Dakota tacked on an order of chicken noodle soup. "It's for my personal assistant, Maggie," she explained before he could ask her how she could still be hungry. "She's down with a stomach bug." *Speaking of shaky stomachs.* "I need to use the ladies room before we go. I'll be right back. Don't follow me," she added as he shifted. "That'll look weird. Low-profile, right?"

She scooted out before he could argue. That's if he ever argued. Her stomach churned as she hurried toward the restrooms. She needed a second to get herself together. He'd spooked her. Actually she'd spooked herself. Thinking about pissed off parents, made her think of the concert fiasco which made her think of the threatening letter hidden in her purse.

She didn't want to think about that creepy letter or the disturbing threat. She'd declared it a hoax. Some sicko getting his or her jollies by making her twitchy. She would have torn it up if Rusty hadn't insisted she show it to Mac. Given his no-nonsense mentality, she was surprised he hadn't asked her about it yet. She was grateful for the reprieve, only now it was forefront in her mind. It was all she could do not to look over her shoulder as she neared the ladies room.

Her stomach cramped and she broke into a sweat.

Oh, no.

She barely made it into a stall before losing her midnight breakfast. Her stomach convulsed time and again until she had nothing left. She was drained. Lightheaded and sweaty. She was mortified and it only got worse because she heard a voice. His voice.

"Dakota."

"Go away."

Only he didn't. He invaded her space, somehow unlatching the stall door and pressing something cool to the back of her neck.

A soaked handkerchief.

Who carried these things anymore?

She swiped it over her brow, over her mouth. "It's not what you think. I didn't make myself sick. I'm not bulimic." Something, just one of the things, she'd been accused of in the past.

"Can you stand?"

"Of course, I can stand," she snapped.

God, she was embarrassed. She'd been existing on smoothies, fresh fruit, and lean fish. Tiny portions. Measured portions. Just thinking about all she'd eaten tonight, what she'd eaten, and how fast she'd eaten made her queasy all over again. So, yeah, she pushed to her feet, but she was shaky and she wobbled and he caught her. Instead of thanking him, she slapped away his hands.

"I've got this," she said, moving to the sink to rinse out her mouth before straightening her spine and striding back into the café.

What if someone finally recognized her, snapped a phone shot, and plastered her face all over social media? She'd rather make it out the front door under her own steam than be half carried out by her bodyguard, giving the impression that she was too drunk or whacked to make it on her own. She'd been down that road about a hundred times too many.

Dakota maintained her calm and stride and made it outside without raising a fuss. She made her way toward Mac's car, knowing he was on her heels, feeling pressured, feeling mortified, feeling hounded. *Stalked*. It wasn't just the letter. It was everyone and everything breathing down her neck. Including her mentor, Roger, who after more than a decade of animosity, was suddenly in league with her father.

She was angry and tired, but mostly she felt trapped.

Can't breathe.

She heard the chirp of the doors unlocking and she climbed into the passenger seat, mind racing, lungs burning. "The soup."

Ice Man cranked the ignition. "What?"

"The chicken soup. Maggie's soup. Where is it?"

"Forget the soup, Dakota. I'm taking you home."

"Not without the damned soup! Get the soup, MacDermott! She's sick and I...I..."

"I'll get the soup. Stay here. Lock the doors. Rusty programmed my number into your phone. Get it out now." He waited until she had it in her hand, before opening his door. "If any one even nears this car, you call me."

He hurried out, hurried off, and the pressure in Dakota's head and chest swelled because he was coming back. And he'd want to talk. About the letter. About her puking. Monitoring and manipulating. Breathing down her neck.

She needed a break. She needed space. She needed to fly.

Ramped on adrenaline, Dakota slid into the driver's seat, revved the engine and peeled into the night at breakneck speed.

Freedom.

Four

Wyatt was five feet from his rental when the tires spit gravel and Dakota as good as gave him the finger with a pair of fading red tail lights. What the...

Another car peeled into the dust she'd left, braking in front of Wyatt. "Get in!"

Acting on instinct, he jumped into the black sedan, still closing the door as the driver gave chase.

"Losing Dakota first night on the job. That's gotta hurt," he said, spectacled eyes locked on the road as he punched the gas. "Don't worry, Mr. MacDermott. Your secret's safe with me. Unless she rolls that sucker and ends up in the hospital. Then I'll have to kick your ass."

"You could try," Wyatt said. Although he deserved some sort of blowback for this rookie mistake. "You her chauffeur?" A natural conclusion, given the car, the man's familiarity, and the fact that Wyatt hadn't seen him with the partying entourage.

The conservatively suited, older man nodded, concentration on the road, gnarled fingers flexing on the wheel as he made a sharp right onto a narrow gravel road. "Dammit, honey. Slow down," he mumbled to the taunting taillights of the rental. "Name's Luther Jones," he said to Wyatt.

"Appreciate the lift, Luther."

"It's what I do. And, oh, hey, don't call her," he added as Wyatt palmed his phone. "She won't talk and drive at the same time. Had an accident like that once and she tends not to forget. Anything," he added in a cryptic tone.

Wyatt replayed the scene. Him walking out of the café, toward his car. Alone. No one else around. No immediate threat to Dakota. Nothing to prompt a panicked escape. Even now, for as far as Wyatt could see, this car and the rental were the only two vehicles in sight.

"Maybe she thinks we're paparazzi," Wyatt said. "Hang back a little. See if she slows down."

Luther slowed.

Dakota didn't.

"So much for that tactic." Luther accelerated hard to tighten the gap. "Lemme catch up. When she sees it's me, she'll pull over."

"Dakota prone to late night joy rides, Luther?"

"Dakota suffers sporadic emotional breakdowns. I'm guessing we're experiencing one right now. Mr. Mitchell sensed something building. That's why he told me to tail you. Not that I'm spying. Just consider me back up."

Wyatt considered the man a blessing. He'd been in the right place at the right time and he was a helluva driver. Wyatt knew from his research that Luther hailed from Los Angeles, yet he navigated these dark and unfamiliar roads at high speed like a native dragster.

Dakota, on the other hand, fishtailed on the gravel as she roared through a tight curve.

"Oh, shit," Luther said as she spun out in front of them, a cloud of dust and gravel obscuring the already limited view.

Lurching into Luther's side, Wyatt commandeered the wheel and jammed his own foot to the brake, swinging the sedan away from the on-coming wreck. They slid to a full stop just as the rental sailed into a cornfield.

"Damn," Luther rasped as Wyatt launched his body out of the car, onto the road, into the field.

Pitch goddamned black except for the headlights shining into a sea of swirling dirt and damaged stalks. Wyatt wrenched open the driver's door, grateful the car hadn't flipped, grateful the airbag had deployed.

Grateful to hear a feminine groan of distress.

"Dakota." Heart pounding, he eased her back into the seat, checking for blood, checking her pulse.

"I'm okay. I'm fine. I'm... Ow," she complained as Wyatt maneuvered her from the car.

"You're lucky to be alive," he said, refusing to feel bad if all she'd suffered was intense bruising—which is what he'd surmised so far.

"Oh, man. Oh, hell," Luther said as he stumbled into the field. "She okay?" he asked as Wyatt lifted her into arms. "Dakota?"

"I'm fine," she rasped. "I'm... Luther? Why are you here? Oh, God. Don't tell Van."

Luther, who looked a little shell shocked, glanced at Wyatt. "Should I call an ambulance?"

"Don't call anyone!" Dakota snapped, sounding more panicked than angry.

"I think we're good," Wyatt said as the wide-eyed chauffeur adjusted his cockeyed Buddy Holly glasses. "See if you can get this car back up on the road. You," he said in a firm voice to Dakota, "be still."

He carried her to the luxury ride, which was now parked safely on the side of the road, and placed her gently in the backseat. The air pulsed with tension and adrenaline and the persistent chirps of crickets or locusts or some other damned farm bug.

Wyatt had been on automatic. Now he wrestled to stay in lockdown. Dakota wasn't all that tiny. Why did she feel so tiny, so fragile, so soft? Why did his heart stop when she met his gaze? When he saw a fleeting jumble of fear and relief?

She'd acted irresponsibly. She deserved a shake, not a hug. Somehow he resisted both urges. Aided by the interior light, he double checked for cuts and broken bones.

"Did you feel threatened?" he asked. "Back at the café. Did something spook you?"

"I couldn't breathe. I needed to fly. I... Stop fussing," she groused, looking embarrassed now as she dodged his hands and wilted against the seat. "Had the wind knocked out of me, that's all."

He wanted to give her hell. Instead he took off his jacket and finessed it over her shoulders. Eighty and humid and she was shivering.

"I'm sorry about your car," she said in a sudden and surprisingly smaller voice.

That hint of vulnerability tested Wyatt's steely walls. He'd sensed the same fragile tenor twice in the café and again when she'd insisted he return for the medicinal soup. Although maybe her concern for her assistant had merely been a ploy to snag his wheels. The possibility magnified his already foul mood.

"*I needed to fly.*"

What kind of spoiled-ass nonsense was that?

Instead of accepting her apology, Wyatt addressed her actions. "That immature stunt could have ended in your death. Or Luther's."

Buddy Holly was good, but Wyatt was better, and it had been Wyatt's razor sharp reflexes and experience that had saved them from ramming into Dakota as the rental spun in their direction. Wyatt didn't spell it out but he shelved his poker expression long enough to betray his thoughts.

"Point made," was all Dakota said before curling into a ball in the far corner.

In his mind he closed the distance, softening his verbal censure with physical comfort.

Sheer will kept him rooted. Reassuring her until she stopped shivering not only struck him as unprofessional but dangerous. She twisted him up. He didn't like her yet he ached to touch her, to stroke her, to kiss her, to... Oh, yeah. This was bad.

"I'm not the man for this job. First thing tomorrow, I'll arrange for a replacement."

He'd never bailed on a job in his life and he hated breaking a promise to Rusty, but this had disaster written all over it.

Disgusted with himself, Wyatt eased out of the spacious sedan as Luther steered the grinding rental back onto the road. He rolled down the window as Wyatt approached.

"Some scratches and dings. Nothing major," he said. "Except that scraping noise. Not sure what that's about. Bottom line, it'll make it to the house. It's actually not too far from here." He tossed Wyatt a set of keys. "You take Dakota in my car. I'll follow, but I'm taking it slow in deference to that scraping. Know where you're going?" he asked then rattled off directions.

"I owe you," Wyatt said to the man, reconsidering his former intent to downsize the entourage by dismissing the chauffeur.

"Just get her back safe," Luther said. "*I* owe her."

* * *

He was quitting.

Badass protection specialist, Wyatt MacDermott had been in Dakota's company for less than two hours and the man was washing his hands of her. No matter how many feathers she'd ruffled over the years, no one had ever thrown in the towel. Oh, sure, Roger had fired a few incompetents and some people had moved on to other gigs, but no one had ever walked away from her fame and wealth simply because she'd ticked them off.

Truth was, for the most part, Dakota wasn't that bad. She had bad moments, but she wasn't a horrible person. Anyone who spent a decent amount of time with her picked up on that truth. Everyone put up with her quirks. Everyone stuck around for as long as they could because of who she was and what she could offer them. Being in her circle opened up a world of opportunities.

Even now.

Granted she was a tarnished, faded star but her established fame still wielded power. If she nailed this comeback concert, more shows would follow. She'd be rolling in money and attention. More offers. More potential. It's why Roger had been able to attract one of the industry's hottest choreographers. It's why six of the youngest and fiercest dancers in Los Angeles hadn't balked at holing up in a no name Midwestern town for a two-week crash rehearsal.

Everyone wanted a piece of Dakota Breeze.

Everyone except for Wyatt MacDermott.

His resignation baffled her already dazed brain. His cold demeanor cut to the quick. His silence...

His silence was torture.

Mostly because it left Dakota alone with her brutal thoughts.

She spent the short ride to her temporary home chastising herself a million times over for stealing and wrecking her bodyguard's car.

"That immature stunt could have ended in your death. Or Luther's."

Why hadn't Ice Man included his name in that short but lethal reprimand? If Luther had lost control of his ride, Mac would have suffered the consequences as well. Her gut knotted just thinking about it. She'd acted impulsively and more often than not bad things happened in the wake of erratic whimsy.

Dakota hadn't meant to put anyone in danger—including herself. She'd crumbled under pressure, but then for a moment, a brief blessed moment, she'd been in control. Racing into the night, turning or veering or accelerating at will. No one telling her what to do, how to dance, how to sing, what to eat, what to wear. No one breathing down her neck.

No one to disappoint.

Then she'd seen the headlights on her tail. She thought about the letter. The threat. And suddenly she was spinning.

Everything from that point until the moment Mac carried her to Luther's leased car was a blur. At least her latest fiasco had happened in the dead of night on a deserted road. No paparazzi. No rubbernecking motorists. No chance of another embarrassing Dakota Breeze episode making the front page of a tabloid.

Regardless, Dakota knew she'd be thinking about this mishap for days. Obsessing over her reckless behavior. Kicking herself for buckling under pressure. She'd devoted the last year to therapy. She'd found calm in relative obscurity, something she used to fear. Then Roger had joined with her dad, a man she'd been estranged from for years, and together they'd pushed for this comeback. Day-by-day, Dakota felt the pressure building. The pressure to impress, to bolster their flagging finances, to salvage her tattered reputation, to appease her disappointed fans.

Everyone assured her she'd feel stoked once she got back to what she loved—performing in front of a live audience. So far all she felt was dread. Rehearsals were frustrating and, at times, depressing. Nothing came easy. Not even her signature dance moves. And the singing... No wonder Van insisted she lip sync to tracks. She couldn't make it through three lines without running out of breath or sliding off key.

The more she floundered, the harder she tried. Her pride wasn't the only thing at stake.

Then that damned letter had arrived in the mail, at Starstruck—her supposed safe haven—and tonight the lid had blown off her brewing anxiety.

She needed to get a grip. She needed to conquer her fears instead of giving them power. No running. No hiding. No buckling. She needed to address the insidious culprit twisting up her focus. She could manage the performance anxiety. She could. But that letter...

"You asked if I felt threatened," Dakota blurted into the dark. "If that's why I took off. That was part of it, yes."

Now instead of annoying, she found Mac's silence a blessing. With him in the front seat and her in the back, with his eyes on the road and not on her, she found the will and nerve to confront what she'd been denying for two days running.

"Someone wants me to cancel this show," she hurried on. "A concerned parent. A vengeful sibling. Someone who remembers me as a teen pop queen and considers me a bad influence on a loved one. Someone who heard about my comeback plans even though my team hasn't made an official announcement. Someone who learned I'm in Kramer and rehearsing at Starstruck.

"I know Rusty told you about the letter," she said to the back of Mac's head. "I told her it was nothing. That I get notes from crackpots all the time. Mostly I said that to make her feel better. I haven't gotten a letter like that in years. I rarely get letters anymore, period. Fans and haters alike have taken to social media as their form of communication. Not that I'm inundated on that score either. I fell off the grid last year when I stopped giving people something to talk about— good or bad. You can imagine my shock when Rusty handed me that envelope."

Dakota eyed her purse and the letter within like a ticking bomb. "I've spent the past two days trying to convince myself that that letter was a nasty prank. I have enough on my plate without having to deal with some vengeful lunatic. Then you showed up and gave validity to that damned threat. A dozen *what ifs* crushed my denial. What if the threat's real? What if some nutjob takes a potshot or plants a bomb—in the house, under the car, at the club? What if someone else gets caught in the crossfire? Luther? Maggie? Van? Rusty? I couldn't bear it.

"*Crawl back into your hole,* the letter said. I wish I could, but I can't. Too many people are counting on me. Counting on this concert and a potential tour. I buckled tonight, but it won't happen again. It would be easier, I think, if I knew you had my back. I know you came for Rusty, but I'm asking you to stay for me."

She palmed her aching chest, fought for an even breath as Mac steered the sedan through the gates to her temporary residence. She hadn't meant to spew or to beg. She didn't want his pity.

But she did want him.

For all his indifference, he made her feel safe. At this point she'd welcome anything, even the company of Ice Man, to minimize her stress. Stress messed with her concentration and judgment, undermining her on-stage performances and her pursuit of private serenity.

Feeling exposed and raw, Dakota pushed her agenda. "So are you with me or not?"

He didn't respond. Of course, he didn't respond. The man was a freaking robot.

The car stopped just shy of the house and, with a white-knuckled hold on her purse, Dakota pushed open her door. Her shoulder sang with the effort, but she didn't groan or complain or even wince. Mac was right. She was lucky to be alive.

She blocked his cold rejection from her mind, focused on Maggie. She needed to check on her ailing assistant and she didn't want to compound matters by looking like a frazzled mess.

A startled scream stuck in her throat as her new bodyguard backed her against the car.

"One," he said, spearing her with steely grey eyes, "You don't move without telling me first. Two: As soon as we get in the house, I want that letter. Three: I say jump, you jump. I'm talking unflinching trust, Dakota."

It was the most he'd said to her since they'd met and even though he'd done nothing but issue arrogant orders, a strange sense of calm snaked through her tense being. Pinned between the tank of a car and her broad-shouldered bodyguard, Dakota held his gaze and raised onto her toes, her mouth a breath away from his own. "For me to jump, MacDermott, I need to know something other than ice flows through your veins."

And with that she indulged in one last impulsive act. She pressed her lips to his, anticipating rejection. Anticipating Antarctica.

Instead, he blew her away, melting her bones with a deep, searing kiss. His touch, his taste, his passion dazed her far more than any spinning car. Who could think straight with his strong hands exploring her curves? With his massive erection raging between them?

Dakota gave over to the intensity, the wonder, the mind-blowing melding that obliterated morality. Just shy of her jumping his freaking bones, Mac cooled her jets by backing away.

"Now you know," he said as he reverted to professional indifference. "And if you're smart, you'll leave it at that."

Five

Kramer, IL
Sunday, June 14, the morning after the meltdown

"It's five in the morning, Mac. What the hell?"

"I need a forensic analyst. Who do we know in Chicago?"

"Tell me you didn't take a freelance gig."

"It's a favor for a friend."

"A friend in Chicago."

"Close enough." Wyatt dragged a hand down his scruffy jaw. He'd given up on sleep. His brain wouldn't shut down and his senses were on full alert. He could lie in bed, obsessing on his impractical attraction to Dakota or he could get the ball rolling on identifying her tormentor.

"I need this done on the QT, Ian." Phone pressed to his ear, Wyatt rolled into a sitting position and switched on his bedside lamp. "Fingerprints. DNA. Whatever it takes to get a match. It's a letter. Possible death threat. Definite intimidation."

"Content?"

Wyatt glanced at the letter laying open on the nightstand. Dakota had given it to him just after delivering the soup

31

(which had somehow survived the drive) to her ill assistant and just before showing him to his room and bidding him a terse goodnight.

"The good mourn your evil existence," he read aloud. "Crawl back into your hole, foul breeze, or suffer my wrath."

"That's it?"

Enough to alarm Rusty. Enough to distress Dakota. Enough to prompt Wyatt into making this call.

"Handwritten?" Ian went on. "Typed?"

"Magazine clippings of random letters," Wyatt said, tearing his thoughts away from the woman sleeping in the next room. "Arranged in that message and glued to stock vellum."

"Clichéd."

"Creepy. Resembles a young girl's collage. Fancy letters. Pastel colors."

"Innocent visual for a vitriolic message."

"Used the same method on the envelope," Wyatt said. "First name only. No mailing address or stamp. Mixed in with the mail. Easily mistaken for a fan letter or innocuous invitation."

"Fan letter, huh. So we're talking a celebrity? You don't... Unless... Oh, hell, Mac. Are you in Kramer? This friend. Is it Rusty?"

No use skirting the truth. Ian was trustworthy and Wyatt needed help. "I'm here because of Rusty, yes."

"Someone's threatening the woman of your dreams? I'd say I'm surprised you sound this calm, but I'm not."

Wyatt had signed on with B.O.S.S. due to a strong referral from Rusty. He'd developed a firm and fast friendship with Ian and though Wyatt had never confessed his infatuation with Rusty Ann Baker, his boss was an intuitive son of a bitch. As always, Wyatt let the ribbing slide.

"The letter wasn't directed at Rusty," he said. "But she's potential collateral damage. The target is a friend of hers and that friend is utilizing Starstruck to rehearse in secret. The letter was mixed in with the club's mail."

"But there was no mailing address on the envelope. Just a name," Ian reiterated. "No stamp. Meaning whoever wrote it had access to the local postman or to Starstruck itself. Which suggests your potential attacker is local. If not homegrown, then lurking in the vicinity."

Another point that had dogged Wyatt throughout his restless night.

"Threat assessment?" Ian asked.

"Level four. Maybe three. I'm fresh on the scene. I'll have a better handle by the end of today." He needed to speak to Dakota at length and in earnest. Had she received any other threats? In what form? How recently? He needed a list of everyone who knew of her present location. Anyone who knew about this comeback venture.

"Are you going to kill the suspense or leaving me hanging?" Ian asked. "Who's the VIP?"

Wyatt worked his stiff shoulders, gaze locked on the thin wall separating him and Dakota. As if he had x-ray vision, as if he could see her sleeping soundly in her bed. It didn't take much to imagine. Her smoking hot body was branded on his brain along with her scent and taste.

Kissing Dakota. Rationalizing that bonehead mistake was like wishing the sky green.

He'd taken what she'd offered. No hesitation.

He'd been too amped, too tempted, too affected by her damned rambling, yet somehow heartfelt speech. He'd kissed her hoping to slake his desire. A professional breakdown that resulted in an epiphany: The attraction went both ways and it burned like a wildfire—fierce and unchecked.

Rather than analyze the absurdity of fate, Wyatt wrestled his lust into lockdown.

It helped if he focused on the past. On the grudge. A petty weapon, but hell, whatever works.

Since he'd been aware of every sound throughout the night, he knew she'd yet to leave her room. Plus, he could sense her. He rarely felt this physically attuned to a principal. Intriguing and uncomfortable at the same time.

"Seriously, Mac. What's with the mystery? I—"

"Dakota Breeze."

"Holy shit." Dead air then, "Rusty asked you to protect... Did you tell her about Kerry?"

"No." Even though Rusty had been under Wyatt's protection for three intense months, even though they'd remained friendly over the years, Wyatt had kept his family and his family's history vague at best.

"So Rusty has no idea of the awkward position she put you in."

"And there's no reason she needs to know. I can handle this, Ian. You know me."

"Yeah. And as I recall that's why I put you on mandatory leave. To live a little. To find some joy in life as opposed to working endless cases like a fucking robot."

"Ever since you hooked up with your lady love, you've been a real pain in the ass, Ian. Do we have a man in Chicago, or not?"

"What do you think?" Ian blew out a breath. "I'll reach out. Since it's Sunday, we're probably talking tomorrow soonest."

"I'll take appropriate measures on my end," Wyatt said as he stood and stretched. "See what else I can learn. The letter's already been compromised. Handled by both Dakota and Rusty and who knows how many others. Maybe I'll get lucky, narrow the field of suspects by asking the right questions."

"Personal connection aside," Ian said, "I'm morbidly hoping Dakota Breeze is the nightmare she's purported to be. In which case, after this, you'll be desperate for some R&R. A man can only walk on the dark side so long before—"

"Ian?"

"What?"

"Go the hell back to bed."

* * *

Dakota stared up at the ceiling, heart pounding as she heard Mac stirring. Their bedrooms were side-by-side, connected by a shared outer second-story deck. The once private country estate had been converted to a bed-and-breakfast at some point and the renovations had resulted in additional bathrooms, locks on every door, and a few shared amenities. Due to hard times, the owners had bailed and now it was a temporary exclusive rental.

Initially her assistant had occupied the semi-adjoined bedroom, but then Maggie had come down with that stomach bug and Van had insisted she move to a room downstairs. Actually, he'd wanted to move her to the house down the road, the secondary rental occupied by Terrance, Luther, Brock, and the dancers, but Dakota had nixed that suggestion. Better to keep the germs contained and besides, Dakota felt protective of her nerdy PA. Maggie wouldn't mix well with the dancers. Why put her in an awkward position? Surely the virus would pass in a day or so.

Since the other bedrooms were occupied by Van and Pauley, and since Mac had insisted on being within hearing distance of Dakota, she'd had no choice but to put him in the room next to hers. On the one hand, she had to admit, it made her feel safe. Unfortunately, it also made her intensely aware of his presence. Like she needed any help in that area. The man had taken up residence in her brain. The sound of his voice, the feel of his hands. He'd kissed her stupid, ignited some sort of freaky mutual passion, and then had the gall to shut it down with a cocky remark.

"If you're smart, you'll leave it at that."

Was that some sort of challenge? Or was he trying to scare her off? Leave it at that or what? I'll break your heart? I'll fuck your brains out? I'll complicate your life? It's not like she hadn't been down all those roads and then some.

Pipes groaned to her left and she knew Mac had cranked up the shower. Another unusual feature regarding this house. These massive side-by-side bedrooms each had a private bath. The walls were fairly thin, so she'd always known when Maggie was making use of the sink or shower. Now it was MacDermott.

Great.

Now all she could think about was Mac in the buff, steam swirling around that hot body as water and soap slid over his toned muscles. She'd gotten a good idea of the man's physique while feeling him up during their heated kiss.

That kiss.

God, how she wished she could forget that knee-melting kiss.

Brain racing, Dakota gave up on falling back to sleep and rolled out of bed with a pained groan. She hurt everywhere. Even her hair hurt. How was that possible?

She switched on a lamp, frowning at the bruises on her wrists and forearms. Badges of stupidity from last night's wreck? Had to be from the airbag. Was her chest bruised as well? Her face? She dreaded looking in the mirror. She dreaded facing Van. And here she'd hoped to keep her meltdown a secret.

Anxious now, Dakota padded slowly to the window and parted the curtains. Dawn was breaking, just barely. She had to get up anyway. Her mornings started early under the guidance of Terrance. A juice smoothie followed by a long run. A light snack followed by weight training or yoga. Then she usually joined Brock and the Darlings for rehearsals at Starstruck.

It was hard enough getting through the intense workouts and rehearsals when she was feeling one hundred percent. Today she felt like she'd been hit by a truck.

"More like a corn field," she said with a disgusted snort. "Suck it up, Dakota. You wouldn't be hurting if you hadn't stolen MacDermott's wheels."

Determined to face this day with dignity, she made a sluggish bee-line to her own private bath. With any luck a hot shower would loosen her muscles and wash away the lingering anxiety instigated by that damned letter. She'd passed it off to Mac, but the message had haunted her dreams.

The good mourn your evil existence.

It flung her back to the years of her evolving image. From bubblegum pop star to provocative performer. The rebellious lyrics of her songs and the sexually suggestive dance moves. Tweens and teens had loved her, idolized her, emulated her. Parents and staunch conservatives had condemned her, labeling her a bad influence, inappropriately racy, vulgar, dangerous. She'd never considered herself any of those things. Roger, her mentor and most trusted friend, had likened her to a modern-day female Elvis Presley. Back in his day, the King had been accused of lewd exhibitionism. Parents had been outraged by his gyrating hips and rebellious rock songs.

While critics shunned her edgy performances, Dakota had considered herself a trendsetter. But then there'd been that concert disaster and the world she'd built came crashing down.

Two dead. Thirty-four injured.

She shook off the horror, put a lid on the memories as she stripped and moved into the shower. It wasn't her fault. She wasn't to blame.

"I'm not dangerous. I'm not evil."

Crawl back into your hole, foul breeze, or suffer my wrath.

Stomach knotted, muscles bunched, Dakota lathered her skin with scented soap.

"I'm not foul."

Yet she cringed every time she and the dancers rehearsed certain segments. At first she'd assumed she was out of practice, but maybe it boiled down to lack of passion. Her heart wasn't in it, so her body rebelled. She felt absurdly lost on stage when she should feel at home.

She'd been toying with an idea, something she'd mentioned to Roger, something he'd shot down. He was all about the sure thing, the solid moneymaker. Tied up in business negotiations he'd hired Van to keep her on track. Last night had been the first night she'd shimmied out from under Van's thumb. And that had been because of Rusty and Mac.

Stepping out of the shower, Dakota ignored her aching muscles as she toweled dry then opted for running clothes that would help hide her bruises. Instead of wallowing in past mistakes she fixated on the future. In addition to negating or squashing the threat against her, maybe Mac could run interference for her secret agenda. That kiss proved he was made of more than steel and ice.

He wasn't willing to be her lover, but maybe he'd be her friend.

Six

After shaving, Wyatt indulged in a long, hot shower. It soothed his stiff body and revved his sluggish mind. As the rest of the house slept, he mused and plotted. By the time he dried off, he'd mapped out his initial meeting with Dakota.

The soft snick of a door prompted him to swap towel for gun.

The last thing he expected as he eased out of the steam was to find Dakota sneaking into his room.

She turned and gasped, although he couldn't say what startled her more. His dick or his Sig.

"What do you shower with that thing?" she asked. "The gun I mean, not..." Cheeks coloring, she shifted her attention from his package to his face. "I thought you'd be showered and dressed by now. I heard you stirring twenty minutes ago."

Wyatt placed his pistol on a nearby chest. "You all right?"

"Fine. I just... I wanted to have a word with you."

"So you broke in through my terrace door?"

"I didn't break in. I have a key." She dangled it in front of her. "You have one to my door, too. It's in that ceramic decanter on the chest. Next to your gun. This was Maggie's

38

room. We used to sit on that connecting deck and sort through business. It's nice out there. We swapped keys for emergency sake."

"Is there an emergency?"

"No."

The longer he stood there in the buff the hotter her flush. Knocking Dakota off-balance suited his purposes. Getting a hard-on did not. But, damn, he found her twice as appealing today as he had last night.

She'd twisted her thick, wet hair into a messy knot and concealed her figure beneath baggy sweats and an oversized zipped hoodie. Her eyes were hidden behind a pair of aviator sunglasses, and her feet were laced into pink running shoes instead of screaming red stilettos. She resembled a freaking sorority girl. Sweet. Sexy. His type with a capital T.

Feeling a twitch, he casually gave her his ass as he pulled on shorts and jeans.

"You're probably wondering why I didn't use the regular door," Dakota blurted. "The floor in the hallway creaks. Between that and knocking on your door... I didn't want anyone to know I was up and around. I wanted to speak with you in private. I could have texted and waited on the deck, but considering it's out in the open, I figured that was some sort of breach of security in your rigid-ass eyes. I knocked on the terrace door," she rushed on, "but you didn't answer, so I let myself in. I thought you'd be dressed by now."

"So you said." Wyatt pulled on a clean shirt, noting once more how his silence caused this woman to ramble. Something that could prove useful when prying for answers. Muting his emotions and his traitorous libido, he turned and regarded his principal with practiced patience.

She shifted her weight, huffed a breath. "Are you waiting for an apology? Fine. I'm sorry I didn't text or call, whatever, to give you a heads up. I suppose I just broke the "don't move without telling you first" rule. My bad."

"You're lucky I don't shoot intruders on sight."

"You're kidding, right?"

He didn't answer one way or the other. "What's on your mind?"

"How this is going to work. You and me. You barked your rules last night, but I should have some input, too."

"Depends on the input."

"Also, I want to talk about that letter," she said, blowing over his response. "I want to know if you think it's a valid threat or not. There's also a matter of my itinerary. It's pretty regimented. Although today is different what with it being Sunday. I want to talk about that, too."

So far this meeting wasn't going as planned.

"In the spirit of trying to honor your stipulations," she went on, "you should know that I'm scheduled to meet Terrance in the kitchen at 7:30 for a smoothie. Then we hit the trail for a five-mile run. I hope you brought sneakers since you'll probably insist on tagging along. Unless you think that letter is a complete hoax and nothing to worry about in which case I'm not in immediate danger so—"

"Do you want a smoothie?"

"What?"

Wyatt flashed back on their late night binge. He remembered her hearty appetite and how her mouth had curved into an almost orgasmic smile when she'd chewed those syrup soaked pancakes. He remembered what she said about being on a strict diet. "Is that what you want for breakfast? A smoothie?"

"Not really. Terrance's smoothies are blended concoctions of vegetables more than fruits. Some are okay. Some are nasty. Something about the texture. But whatever. It's part of the plan and I am losing weight. I'll be damned if I'll squeeze my size-eight body into a size-three costume. Critics are unforgiving and so are body stockings and leather corsets."

Wyatt snuffed the dozen comments crowding his tongue. It wasn't his place to criticize or question her career choices. He was here to protect. Period. But, damn, he had strong opinions regarding style over substance. Not to mention, the pitfalls of body image fixation. He'd been down that road with his sister and at least two former girlfriends. Near as Wyatt could tell, this comeback tour was more of a reboot than a reinvention.

Not your concern.

Narrowing his focus to her safety, Wyatt jumped tracks. "That five-mile run. Take the same route every day?"

She nodded. "A marked trail through the woods, up and over a couple of hills, around a small pond. Total thigh burner, but the scenery's pretty." Twin brows hiked over the rims of her shades. "Does that mean you're coming?"

"It means you're not going. Not on that trail anyway. Maybe not at all. Depending. You were in a car accident last night. I'm guessing you're feeling it today."

"I'm fine."

Her flaming cheeks branded her a liar. Wyatt pressed. "No stiffness? No aches?" He closed the distance between them. "No bruising?"

"Don't worry about my body."

"I'm paid to worry about your body." Technically anyway. He'd be damned if he'd take a penny from Rusty. This was a favor. A pain-in-the-ass-but-doable favor. "What's with the sunglasses?"

"Stop bullying me, MacDermott."

"Ascertaining your welfare and maintaining your wellbeing are part of the job."

Nearly a foot shorter than him, Dakota bolstered her shoulders and hiked her chin. What she lacked in height, she made up for in bravado. "I'm going on that run whether you're on my heels or not. I'm not going to wimp out because of a few aches. I deal with aches all the time. Terrance will report to Van if I bail and then Van will want to know why I'm shirking on my fitness plan. I don't want him to know about last night's meltdown. That means business as usual. If I do what's expected everyone will be happy because it means we're on course.

"Roger, that's my manager," she said after a deep breath, "has a time table and a plan and I need to stick to it. People are counting on me and unless... Just..." She gave him a half-hearted shove. "Dammit, MacDermott. Back off. Let me do what I have to do so I can do what I want to do!"

The diva routine packed more punch when she was glammed up and on show. Right now she came off more desperate than bitchy. Intrigued, Wyatt reached out and pushed her shades to the top of her head.

She frowned.

He stared. Not a stitch a makeup. She was stunning. Even with a black-eye. "How are you going to explain that shiner to Van?"

"I thought... I don't know. A simple lie, I guess. Like I

walked into the wall in the middle of the night on my way to the bathroom."

He lowered the zipper of her hoodie, once again pounding lust into the ground and focusing on the job. "What about these?" Her neon pink sports bra exposed the bruising along her collarbone. He pushed up her sleeves. More bruising on her forearms and wrists. He told himself it could have been worse, but this was bad enough. She'd taken a beating. She had to be hurting. And she was determined to brutalize her body with a five mile run?

"People are counting on me."

It was the second time she'd made a statement like that, suggesting she wasn't entirely self-absorbed. Had he misjudged this woman based on media hype and a highly personal grudge?

Wyatt stared down at Dakota trying to see her as he'd seen her for years. He flashed on the promotional poster that had hung on Kerry's walls during the bulk of her early teens and the countless tabloids featuring the pop sensation throughout her meteoric rise and fall. Where was the cocky sex kitten? The rebellious exhibitionist? The shallow diva with the painted red lips and spider-like lashes?

Instead, he saw what Rusty saw. He saw through the act.

"She's spent her entire life trying to please and impress everyone in her circle, not to mention her fans."

He felt the pressure. Felt her stress.

"I couldn't breathe. I needed to fly."

His preconceptions and objectivity took a hit. He felt like a bastard even though he knew he had sound reason to bear ill will toward the rebellious star who'd motivated his sister to act out with ruinous results. The problem was he was having a hard time reconciling the performer on stage with the woman in his care. Detaching wasn't merely a struggle. It was damn near impossible.

He realized suddenly that he was touching her. Smoothing his thumbs over her bruised wrists.

She stood stock still, saying nothing as his fingers skimmed up her forearms, as he grasped her elbows and gently held her captive.

"I'm not backing off, Dakota. You asked about the letter. Yes, I think there's reason for caution. I'm taking steps to ensure your safety and you're going to help me. You can start by taking the day off. Give your body a chance to heal and us a day to plan for the upcoming week."

He watched her wheels turn. Sensed her wariness and relief, gratitude and a whiff of repressed desire that damn near knocked him on his ass.

"I'll have clear it with, Van," she finally said. "Which means I'll have to cop an attitude."

"Defense mechanism?"

"Secret weapon. There's no reasoning with that man."

"So fire him."

"I can't."

"Why?"

She looked away then looked down at his hands. He still had a grip on her arms and he'd shifted closer—a breath away from a lover's embrace.

She met his gaze and his heart pummeled his ribs. He wanted her. In his arms. In his bed. It went deeper. The need. But he refused to go there. It made no sense and screamed of disaster. He focused on the physical. He could control the physical. Maybe.

"I'm getting mixed signals, MacDermott."

"I know." Last night he'd pushed her away. Now he was tempting the devil.

"Are we going to do something about it?"

"Wouldn't be smart."

"Do you always play it smart?"

"Always."

"Not me."

"I've noticed."

"Maybe I should fire *you*. Then we could just do it. Get it out of our system and move on. That's what's holding you back, right? Professional ethics?"

"That's part of it."

"What's all of it?"

He didn't say. Couldn't say. His reasons were no longer clear and he didn't want to drag Kerry into this. Just thinking about his sister, forever hindered due to an injury she'd sustained at Dakota's infamous disastrous concert, messed with his head. "Rusty asked me to shield you from existing or potential stress."

43

She blinked, laughed. "You think our hooking up would cause me stress?"

"Eventually."

"Wow. Are you that arrogant? Or that sensitive?"

He held her gaze, knowing he was falling, marveling that he was falling. Why her? Why now? "It's complicated."

"Are you married?"

"No."

"That's something, I guess." She dropped her forehead to his chest, blew out a breath. "This is twice now that you've revved me up and shut me down. I don't like it."

"That makes two of us."

She tipped up her face, her luminous green eyes sparking with equal measures of frustration and vulnerability. "For the record I don't sleep around—in spite of what the tabloids say. In fact, I haven't been with anyone, sexually, for over a year. I can't believe I'm telling you this. I just don't want you to think... I didn't come in here for sex. I came for... I need a favor. I need—"

He kissed her. He didn't have any words and she was killing him with every revelation. So he kissed her, easing his longing and doubling his misery. Cursing himself as a hypocrite and a fool as she gave over. His heart thudded slow and hard. His blood burned and his cock throbbed, but he took it slow. Mindful of her injuries. Aware of their surroundings. Of the people sleeping in this house and the possible stalker potentially lurking outside.

Dakota broke off, eyes wide as she backed away. "Sexual attraction is one thing but that... this... This is dangerous."

An intense emotional connection. He felt it, too. Shades of star crossed lovers. What the freaking hell?

"This is crazy," she said.

He couldn't argue that.

"We're a terrible match. I don't know anything about you, MacDermott, but I know we'd mix like oil and water. It could get ugly. I don't want ugly."

He smiled a little, hoping to break the tension. She was wired tight. He was wired tight. The urge to pull her back into his arms was strong. The urge to lay her back on his bed was even stronger. He knew without a doubt they were going down that road. Not now. But soon.

Something about this woman blindsided Wyatt, knocking his judgment and actions off kilter. She challenged his professionalism. She stoked his primal instincts. He anticipated a total clusterfuck, yet did nothing to avoid it. Instead, he stepped out of the frying pan and into the fire, Ian's laughter roaring in his ears. "Name your need."

Seven

"What's up with the sunglasses? I know you're not drinking anymore," Rusty said, "so it can't be a hangover."

"Surprised it took you this long to ask." Accompanied by Mac, Dakota had arrived at Starstruck just before noon. He'd split off to canvas the club. She'd followed Rusty up to her office. They'd been talking for more than fifteen minutes now and she'd yet to remove her gauzy shrug or dark shades. Dakota had no intention of revealing her bruised arms, but she decided to risk the shiner. She was asking some pretty big favors. Her friend had a right to look her in the eyes.

Perched on the edge of a leather club chair, Dakota pushed her sunglasses to the top of her head.

Rusty noted her left eye with a sympathetic hiss. "That had to hurt. What the hell?"

"Stupid accident. My fault. No big deal." Dakota barreled over this moment the same way she'd skirted talk of Mac. "I feel like a pain-in-the-ass, asking you to keep yet another secret, but if this trial run, for lack of a better phrase, goes well I'd like to..." She trailed off, a buttery croissant and two cups of coffee churning in her stomach compliments of Mac. "Let's just see how it goes," she amended, "and I'll take it

46

from there. I really appreciate this, Rusty."

"Not a problem."

"Are you sure the guys won't mind?"

"Why would they mind, honey? You want to sit in. One song. People, many who can't carry a tune in a bucket, sit in with the band every Wednesday night. Bathwater Funk is used to winging it. Hell, they like winging it."

Adrenaline zinging, Dakota pushed out of her chair and started to pace. Mac had afforded her a few private minutes in the company of her friend, but he'd be watching when she got on stage with the house band. He'd be watching and listening and judging. Part of her welcomed his presence—a warped sort of challenge to bring it on strong. Even though she wasn't doing this to impress him, she *wanted* to impress him.

She could almost hear her therapist tsking. Old patterns. Caring too much about what other people think. But somehow this was different. She didn't feel pressured as much as inspired. She couldn't make sense of it in her own mind let alone explain it to someone else. She only knew she was more determined than ever to prove that there was more to her than provocative theatrics.

I'm not evil. I'm not foul.

I'm not a bed-hopping slut.

She'd held it together all morning, but it hadn't been easy. Mac was right. He added to her stress. Considering he'd unraveled her thoroughly with a kiss, she couldn't imagine how she'd feel if they made love. Something powerful lurked between them. Something she couldn't afford to explore. Not with her finances and career hanging in the balance.

"Seriously," Rusty said in the wake of Dakota's silence. "The guys won't blink an eye when I walk you onstage."

"Except this isn't Open Mic night," Dakota blurted. "It's the one rehearsal day they've been allowed all week, thanks to me and my crew. I inconvenienced your band by hogging the stage every day for the last week and now I'm crashing their rehearsal."

"Monopolizing the stage was Van and Brock's call," Rusty reminded her, not that Dakota needed reminding. She'd been awarded minimal input on this entire comeback scenario. "You wanted to rehearse on the dance floor," Rusty went on, "Brock and Van insisted on using the stage."

"Which meant your musicians had to move their equipment at the end of every night in order to make room for me and my dancers. Which meant they had to arrive an hour before their first set every night to put their gear back in place. Which means, I, we, added to their workload. And now I'll be putting them out again."

Rusty didn't comment, causing Dakota to falter in her tracks. She turned and focused on her friend, who pushed out of her chair, perching instead on the corner of her impressively organized desk.

"Are you worried my guys will cop attitudes? They won't. They're professionals." Rusty smiled. "Plus, you're my friend. They know that. Even Ray, who can be a cocky SOB, won't dis you at the risk of pissing me off."

"He's the keyboardist, right?"

Rusty nodded. "Q—Quinn's— on the drums, Connor's on bass, Emmett's the guitarist and Todd's on lead vocals. They're good guys, Dakota, and crazy talented musicians. Do you have a song in mind? Is it one of yours? Something new? Do you have sheet music?"

"No. No sheet music. And it's not an original, it's a cover tune. *Sweet Dreams*."

Rusty scrunched her brow. "By the Eurythmics?"

"By Patsy Cline. I know it's not as popular as *Crazy* or *I Fall to Pieces*, but do you think the guys might know it?"

"Ray knows at least four bars of every song written. Only a slight exaggeration," Rusty added with a smile. "Do you know your key?"

Dakota nodded.

"A chick singer who knows her key. The guys will be impressed. Plus, it's not *Crazy*. Great song, but they get requests for it all the time. Along with *I Will Survive* and *Freebird*. Better them than me," she said with a snort then angled her head. "Not for anything, but *Sweet Dreams* is a huge departure from your normal fare, Dakota."

In other words, it took chops to pull off that kind of rangy ballad. "I know. That's part of the reason I picked it. I had, have this idea, but I don't want to pursue it if I can't pull it off."

Dakota had the sudden urge to spill her vision. Rusty

wouldn't laugh like Roger. Although she might scoff. Rusty had seen Dakota in action during recent rehearsals. She'd heard her struggling to sing her former hits—formulaic pop/rock songs with simplistic melodies. She had every right to be skeptical about Dakota's singing abilities. Dakota was skeptical, too. "I'm not thrilled about this comeback concert."

"I had a feeling."

"I've changed. I've grown. I'm not comfortable with resurrecting the old me."

"Then why do it?"

"We need the money."

"We?"

"Me," Dakota said as she resumed her pacing. "My team. My dad."

"Your dad's back on board? Does that mean you two mended bridges?"

"It means Dad and Roger joined forces and they're a formidable team."

"I can imagine," Rusty said, then sighed. "So instead of pulling you in two directions, they're pooling their influence. Pushing you to do something you don't want to do in order to line their pockets."

"And mine," Dakota said. "According to my accountant, years of reckless spending have crippled my finances. I don't know how I managed it, but I pissed away more than three-quarters of my fortune."

"Are you sure you're solely to blame? You wouldn't be the first celebrity ripped off by managers and accountants. As for your dad, he's notorious for his excessive taste and spending. He made his own bed, Dakota."

She knew that. But it didn't stop her from feeling bad about his present hard times. It didn't erase the fact that she'd wronged him when she'd kicked him to the curb all those years ago in order to benefit from Roger's marketing genius. "I wouldn't have hit it big to begin with if not for Dad. I owe him."

"That's a matter of opinion."

"I'm not bailing on this concert and potential tour," Dakota said. "I just wish it was a breakout instead of a comeback. A reinvention instead of a rehash."

"This was before your time, but like when Linda Ronstadt

surprised her rock fans by recording an album of jazz standards."

Dakota's pulse revved. "Exactly. Performing outside of the box. Broadening horizons and thereby your fan base. I can name half a dozen country stars who crossed over with pop hits and vice versa. I mentioned this to Roger, but he thinks it's too risky. He said it's like starting all over."

"What do you think?"

"I don't mind starting over, but I don't want to put myself out there if I'm not up to snuff. I think I have it in me, Rusty. If I could focus on my voice, on the song, instead of the dances. Brock did an amazing job of combining my signature moves with his innovative choreography, but it takes everything I have physically and mentally to come even close to nailing the sequences. Forget having the stamina and control to sing live. Worse, I'm not enjoying the suggestive tone. Or the music. It used to be fun. Now it's forced. Not to be clichéd, but the thrill is gone."

"A disconnect with the material or your passion or both. I've been down that road a few times," Rusty said. "Sucks to lose the fire."

Dakota shifted toward her friend, took her hand and squeezed. "I knew you'd understand. I guess that's why I'm venting. Sorry about that."

"Don't apologize. That's what friends are for." Rusty returned the squeeze. "So if I'm reading this right, this trial run is your way of reconnecting with your passion and... determining if you're up to snuff?"

"I need to prove something to myself before going out on a limb."

"I didn't realize there was so much riding on this... experiment. That accounts for your anxious mood. Unless... Anything else I should know about?"

Pulse tripping, Dakota fell back. "What do you mean?"

Rusty crossed her arms, narrowed her eyes. "What did Mac say about the letter? You've avoided all mention of him, so I'm guessing it's not good. Avoidance. Denial. It's written all over your aura, girlfriend."

No skirting the issue now. She did, however, resume pacing in order to avoid eye contact. "He said there's reason for caution. We're driving into Chicago after this. Meeting with some sort of expert. Someone who might be able to determine the identity of the sender."

"I like the sound of that," Rusty said.

"MacDermott wants me to scale back on my staff. To send Terrance and Maggie and at least three of the dancers packing. I'm not crazy about cutting them loose with no notice. It's not like they did anything wrong. Although, on the off chance that threat is legit, maybe it's better if they are out of harm's way. I told him I'd think about it. He also wants to switch up my itinerary. Said I'll lessen the chance of an attack if I avoid predictable routes and locations."

"Standard protocol for a security specialist in the face of probable or imminent threat," Rusty said. "That's a road I've been down, too. Seven years ago, to be exact. With Mac." She cleared her throat and lowered her voice. "I've never shared details with you, but I wouldn't be here today if I'd ignored Mac's directive. Yes, he cramped my style, and yes, he was a strong-minded pain-in-the-ass, but he saved my bacon. And ended up impressing me with a couple of life lessons, to boot."

"Did he ever kiss you?"

"What?"

Dakota spun around, hand pressed to her mouth.

Rusty pushed off of her desk. "Mac *kissed* you?"

She hadn't meant to share that detail, but now that she had, she couldn't hold back. "To be fair, I kissed him first. Last night. He put on the brakes. But then this morning..." She palmed her forehead. "I should have called first, but I didn't. I let myself into my room and he was naked and—"

"You saw Mac naked?"

"Have you?"

"No. Jesus." Rusty gawked. "Full frontal?"

"Yeah." It had taken every iota of Dakota's will to tear her gaze from his impressive package. Feigning nonchalance had been an equal challenge. It's not as if she'd never seen a well-endowed man and she sure as hell wasn't a prude, but when he'd emerged from the bathroom, buck naked and brandishing a gun, adrenaline had skyrocketed along with her hormones. There'd been a simultaneous assault on her brain and libido, smoking her senses and reducing her to a rambling idiot.

That he'd seemed unfazed by his state of undress had only rattled her more. While he'd casually chided her for breaking into his room, she'd been forced to endure the glory of washboard abs and sculpted pecs. When he'd turned his back to pull on his briefs, she'd endured further torture. Now his tight ass was branded on her corneas along with his other physical attributes.

Even after he'd dressed, Dakota had fought to slow her pulse. He'd stunned her with actual conversation. Granted, she'd carried the bulk of the banter, but he'd filled the silence. He'd responded to her comments or questions. Mostly. And he'd smiled. Sort of. A slight curve of his hypnotic mouth just before he'd kissed her blind and then asked her to "name her need". Yeah, boy, hadn't that been a loaded request. She *needed* a good ravishing.

"Are you and Mac fooling around?" Rusty asked.

"We haven't slept together, if that's what you're asking. But the potential is there. He's fighting it and I'm wary because...damn, there's something between us, Rusty. Crazy, right? We've known each other less than two days. Hell, we don't *know* each other at all, but when we kiss... I can't explain it."

Rusty jammed her hands in her rear pockets and dropped her chin. "I can't believe this. Or maybe I can." She shook her head. "The question is, is it a talent crush or the real deal?"

"What's that supposed to mean?"

Rusty looked up. "Mac's cool on the surface, Dakota, but the man runs deep. Tread carefully."

Her friend's warning came a day and two kisses too late. "If it makes you feel better, I think we'd make a horrible match."

"For what it's worth," Rusty said as she ushered Dakota out of her office, "I'm not sure I agree."

Eight

Wyatt waited at the base of the spiral staircase as the two women descended from the second floor. Dakota had wanted to approach Rusty privately about singing a song with the house band—something she hadn't wanted Van to know about and something she hadn't fully explained to Wyatt. Something he hadn't argued against because Starstruck was closed on Sundays and it gave him a chance to do an extensive inspection of every room, every hall, every entry and exit point.

His watch told him they'd been in discussion behind closed doors for nearly half an hour. His instincts told him they'd discussed more than an impromptu performance. Rusty caught his eye and her fleeting expression verified his suspicions. She knew he'd been indiscreet. The question was would she pry? And if she did, what the hell would he say?

"The guys are here and tuning up," Rusty said, gesturing toward the stage. "Let's catch them before they get into the heat of rehearsal," she said to Dakota then turned to Wyatt. "Meet me in the audio booth," she said with a smile that worried him more than the business end of a gun. "Be there in a sec."

Wyatt watched as the women moved swiftly across the massive dance floor. A buffed hardwood wasteland—unlike last night when it had been jammed with sweaty, writhing bodies. Now it was just Rusty and Dakota. Two singers. Two performers. Two top-selling recording artists. One had gone out on top. The other down in flames. Two vastly different backgrounds and personalities and yet both had gotten under Wyatt's skin within hours of meeting them. What were the frigging chances?

It's not as if he had a hard-on for the rich and famous. Part of the reason he specialized in VIP protection. He wasn't impressed by status. He was, however, obsessed with the danger VIPs attracted and their influence and impact on the masses. For Wyatt, it wasn't purely about protecting the principal. It extended to anyone in their immediate presence.

Collateral damage.

Kerry had been collateral damage.

Wyatt blamed himself as much as he blamed Dakota and her handlers. He'd distanced himself from his mom and sister because of a beef with his stepfather. He didn't regret the time he'd served in the military, but he did regret ignoring the troubles on his own home front.

Right now the potential trouble was here at Starstruck.

Dragging his hand through his hair, Wyatt focused on the present, scoping the surroundings one last time while moving toward the tech booth—a sectioned off dais with a prime view of the stage.

The club was deserted—except for the five musicians huddled on stage. Bathwater Funk. Hell of a name for a band although, as Dakota had pointed out, a memorable one.

"*Competition's a bitch,*" she'd said. "*Anything that'll help you stand out from the pack—like a unique name—is a bonus. I can tell you from experience Lucy Shaw was not an attention grabber.*"

Shaw. Wyatt connected the name with her first manager. Her father. David Shaw.

She'd thrown him a quick look over the metallic rims of her shades. "*Giving me a stage name was my dad's first stroke of genius. He had a few. Back in the day.*" Then she'd switched subjects, clearly unwilling to discuss her father or her real name.

Lucy.

Approaching the steps on the left side of the stage, Dakota looked back across the dance floor, toward the sound booth. Was she looking for him? Given the dim house lighting he was probably no more than a silhouette. She, on the other hand, was bathed in soft pink and blue stage lighting. She looked sweet and luminous in a long, flowery sundress and a cheery yellow jacket. Her hair was still looped in a messy knot and her sunglasses were firmly in place.

Lucy.

He could see it.

"The guys are running through the chord changes, transposing the key," Rusty said as she unlatched a swinging door and ushered Wyatt up into the booth. "Dakota wants to change up the tempo so that's why she's in a head-to-head with Q. The boys want to do right by her and so do I. They usually make do with floor monitors for rehearsal, but I'm cranking up the house speakers. I want to hear this and I want Dakota to get the full effect."

Wyatt stood aside as Rusty flipped switches and adjusted faders. They were surrounded by amp racks, a massive sound board and an equally complex lighting console.

In addition to accompanying Rusty on a concert tour, several of Wyatt's assignments included special appearances and speaking engagements. In the process of scrutinizing the environment and authorized personnel, he'd become familiar with similar tech gear and a job that required its own brand of specialized expertise.

"When did you master all this?" he asked.

"I married an audio technician, remember? This is Frank's lair. I get a charge out of watching him work, listening to his magic. He's the master, not me. I just know the basics."

"You light up when you talk about him."

She smiled a little as she fiddled with more buttons. "No, I don't.

"Yeah. You do."

She looked over her shoulder. "That bother you?"

"No." Surprisingly, he meant it. Seeing Rusty in person for the first time in years had helped to put his lingering fascination in perspective. He'd loved her once. He loved her still. But not in the way he'd imagined. "I'm happy for you, Rusty."

"I'm glad. And you should be, honey. Frank and I are crazy in love. After a nail-biting stint in the Marines, my son is safe and stateside. And Starstruck is everything I hoped it would be and more. I have a good life, Mac. And you?"

He crossed his arms and relaxed against the waist-high barrier. "If you ask Ian, I don't have a life."

"So you decided to spice it up with Dakota?"

He didn't answer directly because he didn't have a direct answer. He glanced past Rusty to the stage, to the woman testing her microphone. His heart beat slow and hard. He sensed Dakota's anxiety, her excitement. He didn't understand it, but he sensed it. If he was closer, he'd squeeze her hand in reassurance. Even at this distance he noted the slight trembling of her fingers as she removed her sunglasses and adjusted the height of the mic stand. She touched him in ways he couldn't explain. This bone deep attraction, this obsession, was a first for him and it wasn't pretty.

"It's not like you to mix business and pleasure," Rusty barreled on as she hiked the volume and adjusted the lighting. "I should know. I didn't have a clue as to how you felt about me until I was free and clear of danger. Does this mean you're not particularly concerned about that anonymous letter? Showing it to an expert, is that just standard protocol? Should I stop worrying about a stalker and start worrying about you? Do you know how many men have stomped on that girl's heart?"

"Only if I'm supposed to believe what I read in the tabloids." Wyatt shifted. "What's got you so jazzed? This isn't like you." Even in the face of mayhem, Rusty was typically the voice of reason. Calm. Logical. A rock in any crisis.

"Did Dakota tell you why she wanted to sit in with the band today?"

"No."

"There's a lot riding on this performance, Mac. I don't have time to explain it," she said as she settled in the chair behind the consoles. "And I'm not sure you'd understand even if I did."

Music swelled from the stage, from the speakers. Wyatt turned his attention to the band, to Dakota. She'd repositioned the mic stand, moving it closer to the edge of the stage as if putting herself out there and on display. No skimpy costume. No choreographed theatrics. No edgy persona.

No Dakota Breeze.

This was Lucy Shaw.

The air hummed with a symphonic cascade of notes, a short intro that trickled down to one chord. The band droned on that chord, obviously waiting for Dakota to start singing.

"Come on, honey," Rusty said as the music droned on. "Breathe. Focus."

The musicians glanced at one another, a silent exchange that prompted the guitarist to move forward. He spoke close to Dakota's ear.

She nodded, a barely perceptive nod as she licked her lips and tightened her grip on the stand.

"From the diaphragm," Rusty said. "You can do it."

Wyatt moved forward, riveted with anticipation. He found himself rooting alongside Rusty even though he wasn't entirely sure of what he was rooting for.

Then it happened.

Dakota opened her mouth and a rich voice rang out. A high note with a slow warble. She lingered on the opening word—*sweet*—then slid down to the rest of the phrase— *dreams of you*. The drummer kicked in—a slow, bluesy beat—and Dakota dug deep.

Wyatt wasn't familiar with the song, but he could feel every note, every lyric seeping into his soul. The melody was beautiful in its simplicity and yet, even though he didn't have a lick of musical talent, he knew it was a tough song to sing. It took range, stamina, and dead on pitch. But it wasn't Dakota's vocal skills alone that stunned Wyatt. Her performance was electrifying. Her body language and expression. Subtle yet powerful.

Emotional.

His skin prickled as she poured her heart into the country-esque ballad. He'd never seen her like this. Never heard her like this. And he'd heard and seen Dakota in action plenty of times thanks to Kerry.

Where have you been hiding, Lucy? And why?

The song ended as it began, that cascade of notes, the low

drone. And then silence.

Awed silence.

Wyatt would swear the band was as blown away as he was. He could see their dumbstruck expressions from here, and Rusty's, "Holy shit," was practically in his ear.

Dakota lit up with a smile that knocked Wyatt for a second loop.

He dragged a hand down his slack jaw the same time Rusty turned to him, saying, "I can honestly say I have a talent crush. And you, my friend, wow," she said as if reading his thoughts and sizing him up in a heartbeat, "you're positively lovesick."

Nine

Dakota was torn between kicking up her heels and weeping with relief. Nailing that ballad hadn't been easy, but after a shaky start, she'd taken a leap of faith, shucking pretense for raw emotion.

No pre-determined stage blocking. No practiced moves or expressions. Nothing to divide her attention or effort.

She'd focused on her voice.

She'd listened to the music and she'd followed her heart.

Knowing she wasn't being judged by a massive audience or any one person in her inner circle had helped to free her spirit. She'd embraced the support of the musicians, of Rusty, and—although perhaps wishful thinking—even Mac. Positive vibes had sparked from all directions, rippling through her body like a magical spell. Buoyed by their support, she soared.

Dakota rode that high until the very last note, until the music faded.

But then she floundered in the silence—ecstatic and dazed.

The band gathered around her, heaping carefully worded praise. Clearly, she'd surprised them. Hell, she'd surprised herself. Of course, she knew she had a decent voice. But she'd long forgotten the pure joy of singing for the love of it.

The rush was far greater than any musical award, standing ovation, or sizable paycheck.

Now that she'd reconnected with her most basic passion, Dakota felt an almost manic need to protect that treasured gift.

Her father had twisted her natural born talent.

Roger had twisted her talent even more.

And although the mutation had won her fame and fortune, it had cost her true happiness, true love, and any semblance of serenity.

She fairly reeled from the realization.

"Are you okay?" Emmett asked as he gently cupped her shoulder.

Dakota smiled at the guitarist. "As kind as you are talented. I'm fine, thank you."

She swore the man blushed.

The keyboardist snorted and the drummer, Quinn, elbowed Emmett with a good-natured nudge. "Kiss up."

Dakota turned to the lead singer. "Thanks for letting me use your mic, Todd."

"Anytime. Seriously. I know you're keeping your presence in Kramer low key, but you should sit in with us on Wednesday night."

"Yeah," the bassist said. "Give the audience a taste of what you've been hiding."

"I appreciate the offer," Dakota said, relishing their obvious approval, "but I'm not sure that would be wise."

Ray crooked a brow. "Dakota Breeze playing it safe?"

"Dakota Breeze protecting Lucy Shaw. And on that cryptic note," she said with a shy smile, "I'll take my leave. Thanks again, guys."

She hurried off stage, leaving Bathwater Funk to rehearse in peace, and ran into Rusty and Mac midway across the dance floor. Rusty stunned her with a bear hug and, even though it hurt, Dakota ignored her bruises and hugged her friend back.

"I knew you had it in you, honey," Rusty said. "I knew you were good. Just not *that* good. You have to speak up to Roger and your dad."

"I will."

"When?"

"Soon."

Rusty pushed her to arms' length then narrowed her eyes. "You're going to go through with the comeback concert as planned, aren't you?"

Dakota glanced at Mac. She'd looked his way twice now. Waiting for him to compliment her performance or to give some sign, any sign that he'd been impressed by her heartfelt delivery.

He said nothing. Betrayed nothing.

Predictable MacDermott.

His indifference hurt.

She shouldn't care. But she did.

Typical Dakota.

Then she remembered something Rusty said.

"Mac's cool on the surface, but the man runs deep."

Maybe she was misinterpreting his silence. Maybe she'd impressed the hell out of him, but he was too buttoned-up and professional to gush in front of the woman who'd hired him. Maybe he'd compliment her in private.

The man runs deep.

He also runs hot and cold, Dakota thought to herself. Kissing her then pushing her away. *Who needs that shit?*

She'd killed on that stage.

She'd reignited the fire.

She'd had an epiphany.

Two epiphanies.

Pumped with purpose, Dakota focused back on Rusty. "We've taken up enough of your day off and there's that appointment in Chicago. We should go. I can't thank you enough, Rusty. I found what I was looking for."

"Then why aren't you going out on a limb?"

Dakota fixed her gaze on Mac. "Because I've decided to play it smart."

* * *

Since Wyatt's rental was being serviced by a local repairman, Luther was their designated driver and since Dakota wanted to keep her "experimental" performance secret, they spent the majority of the ride to Chicago in relative silence. Otherwise he would have asked her a few direct questions about this comeback concert.

Why aren't you pursuing a recording project that would highlight the beautiful voice I heard today? Why bend to your handlers' vision when you so obviously have one of your own?

None of his damned business, but he was curious. He also wanted to know what Rusty had meant when she said there was a lot riding on that performance of *Sweet Dreams*. He assumed it was something of an artistic nature otherwise why wouldn't he understand?

The longer they rode in silence, the longer his list of questions. They extended beyond her career and crossed over to personal. His interest was unprofessional and the intensity of his curiosity chafed.

"For chrissake Mac," he could hear Rusty say, *"Professional went out the window the moment you stuck your tongue down her throat. The least you could do is get to know her. The real her."*

Then again, if he pried, Dakota would have every right to ask about his life in return. That's not a road he wanted to travel.

Even though his mind kept circling around Dakota's past and future, Wyatt kept his head in the game. He alternated between checking the traffic for a tail and conducting business via his phone. Ian's forensic man, Kyle Burns, had agreed to meet him off-the-clock. They exchanged basics via texting. All Wyatt had to do was deliver the letter. He also checked in with Rusty and touched base with Van Mitchell.

Yes, Dakota's safe. Yes, Dakota's enjoying her day off.

In truth, Wyatt suspected she was pissed. He assumed Luther sensed it too since the man had given up on small talk thirty miles back. At first Wyatt assumed she'd buried her nose in a magazine to avoid off-limit topics—the threatening letter, the secret Starstruck performance. Now he was fairly sure she was avoiding conversation period. With him specifically.

He shouldn't care. But, dammit, he did.

Just when he thought she'd clammed up for good, she set aside the magazine and fussed with her hair.

"I feel like celebrating," she blurted to the back of Luther's head. "After we meet up with MacDermott's friend,

I'm going to indulge in spa time and shopping. Van, task master that he is, designated this as our one day off. I'll be damned if I'll waste it."

She nabbed her phone and texted. "Letting Van and Maggie I'll be out late. Maybe all night. Maybe Van will actually go out and do something relaxing. Pauley's with the dancers. Which means Maggie will have the house to herself. That's a good thing. She's been cooped up in her bedroom for three days."

"That girl should see a doctor," Luther piped in.

"Maggie's quirky, Luther. You know that. She doesn't like attention."

"She's in the wrong business if you ask me. Except you didn't, so forget I said anything." He shot Wyatt a look via the rearview mirror, including him in the conversation—unlike Dakota. "Ms. Breeze takes on misfits now and again," he said. "Like me and Maggie."

"You're not misfits," she argued. "You're just...socially awkward. That said you both excel at your work. Speaking of, you deserve the day off as well, Luther. After you drop us at the designated address, take off and do your own thing. We can cab it for the rest of the day." She afforded Wyatt a fleeting glance over the rims of her shades. "Right?"

"Sure."

Oh, yeah. She was pissed. At him. And she was going to punish him by making him wait in some exclusive spa's reception area while she treated herself to a massage and God knew what else. Not that her battered body didn't deserve pampering, but he could do without the shopping spree after. No doubt someone would recognize her as Dakota Breeze. Then the mania would begin, making his job as a solo protection specialist twice as hard.

"So what are we celebrating?" Luther asked as he navigated thickening traffic.

"My comeback," Dakota said. "And beyond. I can do this, Luther."

"Of course you can, honey. But the question is, do you want to?"

"Absolutely."

Wyatt felt as though they were talking in some kind of code. Kind of like Rusty. He wanted to crack it. He wanted some one-on-one with Dakota. He wanted to ask his long list of questions. He wanted to steal some time as man and woman as opposed to bodyguard and principal. He'd been in her company for less than forty-eight hours and he was completely infatuated. Rusty had nailed it. *Lovesick.*

Jesus.

Knowing Dakota's heart and mind was only half of it. He ached to learn every curve of her body. To finish what they'd started twice. It didn't help that she looked like Sweet Suzy Sunshine in her gypsy-like dress and sandals. He was trying like hell to crank it down a notch.

And losing.

Minutes later, Luther dropped them at Michigan Avenue—also known as Magnificent Mile, an upscale shopping region—and, after a reluctant moment, drove off to enjoy his free time.

Alone at last.

Wyatt would have confronted Dakota then and there on curb, but Burns was waiting. So instead, he finessed her out of the sunshine and into a trendy café. "Order us something to drink," he said after guiding her to the counter and slipping her cash. "I'll be right back."

"I..."

"What can I get for you?" the server asked then directed Dakota's attention to the "specials" chalkboard while listing several other beverage choices.

Wyatt slipped away. Burns caught his eye and the exchange took place in under a minute. Wyatt returned to the counter just as Dakota spun around with two bottles of spring water.

"All those exotic juices and seltzers and you chose water?" he asked with a crooked brow.

"I don't know what you like," she snapped while pushing her sunglasses to the top of her head. "You could have given me a clue."

"Water's fine," he said, placing his hand at the small of her back and nodding toward the door. "Ready?"

"What about meeting the forensics guy?"

"Done."

She blinked and looked around. "Burns was here? You gave him the letter? Why didn't you include me?"

"It wasn't necessary."

"Then why am I here at all?"

"Because I needed to be here and until I determine whether or not you're in mortal danger, we're joined at the hip."

She narrowed those gorgeous green eyes. "In that case I hope you can afford the Drake Hotel because that's where I'm headed."

To make use of a luxury spa, he assumed. Not that he had any intention of personally utilizing the services. "You want to tell me why we're fighting?" he asked as she strode outside and beckoned a taxi.

"We're not fighting."

"The hell we aren't." He opened the back door and slid in beside her, waiting until she'd given the cabbie a destination before pressing on. "You're angry with me because I neglected to compliment your performance."

"I'm angry with myself for giving it a second thought," she said while unscrewing the bottle cap. "Your opinion shouldn't matter. It doesn't matter. I nailed that performance. I felt it to my bones. In my heart. I needed to prove something to myself and I did. That's all that matters. I don't care what you or anyone else thinks of my voice or my style or my...anything."

"That's a lie."

"Maybe." She swigged water then shrugged. "Be that as it may, I'm no longer a slave to approval and adulation."

"Yet you're going ahead with the concert as planned by your management team. Starving yourself to fit into skimpy costumes you don't want to wear, performing songs you have no interest in singing."

"I never said that."

"You as good as said that."

"I didn't think I could pull it off before. A retread of my old self. But now I know different. It's all in the attitude. I'm going to come back, MacDermott, and I'm coming back strong. For the money. For the people who are counting on me. And then I'm going to walk away. For good."

The taxi pulled alongside the landmark hotel and Wyatt struggled to make sense of Dakota's claim as she scrambled onto the sidewalk. He paid the cabbie, catching up to her as she blew through the front door. She navigated the lobby as though she'd been here before. Probably stayed here on one of her tours. A five-star hotel for a one-time star.

Approaching the front desk, she dug in her purse while speaking to the clerk. "One of your suites with the waterfront view, please."

"Mr. and Mrs. MacDermott," Wyatt said, staying her hand and passing the clerk his own credit card.

She didn't argue, but she did raise a brow.

Wyatt signed then pocketed the key and directed his damnable principle toward the elevators.

"Protecting my privacy?" she asked.

"Making my life easier."

"For what it's worth, I was going to sign in as Lucy Shaw. I do know a thing or two about laying low."

"If that's the case, let me guess. Rather than visiting a spa and risking curious stares, you plan on arranging an in-room massage."

She smiled as they hit their upper floor and the doors dinged open. "Feel better?"

A man in her bedroom, a stranger, rubbing oil all over her naked body? Hell, no. "What about the shopping spree?" he asked as they moved down the hall.

"If I'm so inclined after the massage there's always QVC." She sighed as they came to the door of the suite. "Listen, I'm not really interested in celebrating anything. I only said that so Luther would go off and do something fun instead of tagging along and worrying about me. I've been through an emotional and physical wringer lately. Last night's disastrous joy ride didn't help. You, this, us—whatever this is—doesn't help. Now... This is the first time I've been away from my team in over a week. It occurred to me that I could use this day, this night even, to decompress. Hence the room."

Looking weary now, she flattened her back against the wall and crossed her arms. "You were right. I was angry, hurt actually, that you didn't compliment my performance. Not to be dramatic, but that was a defining moment for me. You wouldn't understand—"

"I want to understand."

She angled her head. "Engaging in a heart-to-heart? Doesn't sound very professional."

"It isn't."

She studied him for a long moment, causing his pulse to race like a mother. "You're running hot right now, MacDermott. Historically, in the whole two days I've known you, that doesn't last long. I'm not big on the hot/cold thing."

"Nor should you be."

"Are you always so conflicted?"

"No." He smoothed his thumb over her bruised cheek. "This is a first."

She moistened her lips, held his gaze. "I'm thinking about inviting you inside."

"You're thinking too hard."

"Are you flirting with me, MacDermott?"

"Would you prefer a direct approach?"

"Given our history—"

"All two days of it?"

She smiled and his heart skipped three beats.

"Direct would be nice," she said.

"Okay." He leaned in, searching those gorgeous eyes as he let down his guard. Connecting with the woman who'd stolen his heart with one raw performance. "If I walk through that door, *Lucy*, it'll be as lover, not bodyguard. I want to know you and I want to fuck you. The order doesn't matter."

"Wow. That was direct." She blew out a breath, but she didn't flinch. She didn't blush or play coy. She said, "Okay. My turn. If you walk through that door, whatever happens in this room, stays in this room. No overthinking. No talking it to death. If we do this, we do it knowing it will end badly. Because it will, right?"

He couldn't argue that, so he didn't. His fricking heart lodged in his throat as he waited for her to backpedal.

She took the key card from his hand, slid it into the slot then looked over her shoulder. "Would you like to come inside, Wyatt?"

Ten

As soon as Mac locked the door, Dakota turned and backed him against the wall. "You may not care about the order, but I do. You can ask me anything you want. After," she said while working the buttons of his white shirt. "*Knowing me* could be a total turn off. Considering we're hot and bothered *now* let's do this *now*. I—"

"What happened to not talking this to death?" He reversed their position. Unknotted her shrug.

She opened his shirt. Pressed her lips to his impressive chest while pushing his jacket from his equally impressive shoulders.

He expedited the process, ridding himself of the jacket and shirt while kissing her stupid.

There would be no overthinking this. She could barely breathe, let alone conjure a coherent sentence. She felt the soft fabric of her dress skimming up her body, along with his hands. His mouth played over her cheek, her jaw, her neck, her ear—an endless kiss as he stripped away her clothes and senses.

He broke away long enough to admire her pink bra and thong.

Her skin sizzled as he devoured her form. Bare. Lush.

"Gorgeous," was all he said, yet she read so much more in his eyes.

Your body, your curves—perfect. Size eight? Why would you want to be anything less?

Her heart pounded as he freed her hair of its twisted knot. Her stomach coiled as his fingers skimmed the waistline of her thong. His fingers dipped beneath the satin— a brush, a touch. Fleeting. Teasing.

Frantic with desire, Dakota attacked his belt and zipper. "The last two days have been nothing but foreplay. Let's skip to the main event."

He slowed her efforts, capturing her hands and leaning in to devour her mouth. Pressing her against the wall, kissing his way down her body, biting her nipples through the thin demi-cup, trailing hot kisses down her stomach as he knelt... As he hooked her thong and peeled it down her legs... As he bared her and licked and nipped and suckled her tingling essence.

Feverish now, Dakota closed her eyes, willing her legs not to buckle and her pulse not to cease. She trembled and moaned as he tongued her toward orgasm. As he teased and tortured and ... "Yes!"

Her body tensed and bucked. She climaxed and shuddered. Shuddered and sighed. Her vision blurred and she smiled because, damn, that was good. That was great. That was, "Amazing."

She wilted a little as he rose, but he held her steady, his own need raging as he pressed against her, kissing her shoulders, her neck. She caught him glancing toward the bedroom. "No," she said. "Here. Now." She'd never make it that far. She was too hot, too randy, too desperate.

She'd been worked up before, lots of times, but never like this.

The connection—that emotional something that she didn't fully understand and didn't want to feel because it was frightening and thrilling and unquestionably dangerous— magnified every sensation, every reaction.

What would happen if they took this to bed? Would it intensify the intimacy? Could she savor the wonder and then leave it behind?

Whatever happens in this room, stays in this room.

Could she be that worldly? That calculated? That controlled?

"Overthinking," he said close to her ear. Finessing her body—skin to skin, soft curves to hard plains.

He shucked his jeans and shorts and suddenly she was in his arms, her legs wrapped around his waist as he slid deep. As he rocked her against the wall—hard and slow. Hard and fast.

The friction. The motion.

That freaking connection.

She gasped and moaned and begged.

She soared.

Then with one last plunge she climaxed, riding a tsunami of sexual euphoria.

It went on forever, messing with her mind. *Messing with her heart.* And she realized, even in this fog, this daze, this rapture, that she'd fallen for MacDermott even without falling into bed.

"You okay?"

No. She was not okay. Head resting on his shoulder, she managed a lie. She nodded. He was still inside of her, filling her, stretching her. Her insides coiled knowing this wasn't over. But instead of taking her again—here, now—and finding his release, he eased out and away, lifting her into his arms and carrying her across the room.

"Considering this may be our one and only time," he said as he swept back the bedcovers and placed her on the cool sheets, "I'd like to play out the two dozen fantasies I had about you over the last two days."

Her heart slammed against her chest as he moved over her—naked and powerful and drop-dead handsome. She tried to remember what she had against hooking up in bed with this man then remembered the point was moot. She'd been an idiot to think she was any match for Mac and what had raged between them from the get-go. She'd tried to reduce this moment to "just sex" knowing, deep down that with him, with them, it would never be that simple.

She was in love.

Desperately, achingly in love. And there was no hope for it. For them. She'd stolen this moment thinking it would be enough.

It has to be enough.

Slipping his hand beneath her back, he unclasped her bra, holding her gaze as he bared her breasts. "This could take a while."

"Take your time," she said, trying to sound flirty even as tears of frustration threatened to well. "We've got all night."

* * *

Wyatt had wanted sex and he'd gotten it.

Against the wall. On the bed. In the shower.

He was royally screwed.

In all the ways he'd imagined and in the one way he'd hoped to avoid.

His ability to lock down his emotions had faltered seconds after walking through the door of the suite. The moment Dakota initiated the physical and referenced the emotional.

"Knowing me could be a total turn off."

Her vulnerability seeped into his heart, crippling his defenses, his walls, his will. His mind flashed with a montage of recollections and realizations. Things he'd read—in magazines and on-line. Things he'd heard from Kerry and Rusty and from Dakota herself. They all circled a truth. Dakota's truth or at least her core.

Without asking even one of his several questions he knew she was a good soul who'd been manipulated and influenced by her environment and people she admired. He knew she wanted something beyond what she'd achieved before. He knew she was sensitive and kind, thoughtful and loyal. And he knew her Achilles' heel—the need to please and a fear of rejection.

It explained so much.

Even though Wyatt burned with sincere curiosity regarding the details of Dakota's rocky road, his heart knew enough. It had known the first night. That first kiss had cinched a once-in-a-lifetime bond.

Pure, nonsensical, cupid's-arrow-through-the-heart love.

He hadn't recognized it because he was too grounded and cynical. Too focused and shielded. Too convinced fate couldn't possibly be this twisted.

Now it was balls-out in his face. He was in love with Lucy Shaw and cursed with the mania of Dakota Breeze.

He. Was. Screwed.

Wyatt finished toweling off then pulled on a complimentary robe knowing he had to come clean with Dakota about his sister, knowing this is where things would go bad.

She'd scampered out of the bathroom ahead of him in search of a tube of moisturizer she kept in her purse. She'd also mumbled something about room service. At least they'd be staying in for the night, allowing him to break the news in private. The question was when and how.

He moved into the sitting area expecting to find her slathering lotion or skimming a menu. He found her holding his phone.

"Who's Kerry?" she asked and his blood iced.

"I wasn't snooping," she rushed on as he closed the distance between them. "I heard your phone ring then it stopped. Next I heard the blip of an incoming text. I was bringing the phone to you, thought it might be Burns. Thought maybe he had news about the letter. But *Kerry* showed on the screen, along with *Call me. Miss you. Love you.*"

Wrapped in a matching robe, she looked up at Wyatt with injured eyes. "Is she the reason you said hooking up would cause me stress?"

"Yes. But it's not what you think." He took his phone, laid it on the table next to his gun then took Dakota's hand and pulled her down beside him on sofa. "Kerry's my sister."

"Oh." Her cheeks flushed and her hand fluttered to her brow. "Wow. Okay. That was an embarrassing display of jealousy."

Touched by Dakota's obvious affection, Wyatt dragged a hand through his wet hair. "I'm going to take this as my cue—"

"To remind me that nothing can come of this. Us. I know."

She blew out a breath then met his gaze. "You told me up front that it was complicated on your end. It's complicated on my end, too. I'm obligated to go through with this concert,

Wyatt, and whatever comes of a tour. My dad is struggling financially and I've put a huge dent in my savings. We need the money and this is the surest way to get it. Also, Roger put his reputation on the line, assuring promoters I'd deliver a jaw-dropping performance. That's why I'm here in Kramer, rehearsing in private, getting myself up to speed after years of dragging.

"He's contracted musicians and dancers, technicians and designers," she went on. "Every one of them is counting on me for a job. No one would be surprised if I bailed on the whole thing. In case you haven't kept up with the tabloids over the past several years, I'm famous for sabotaging performances and relationships. I'm also famous now for letting down my fans."

Tears shimmered in her eyes as she clasped her hands in her lap. "I'm sure you know about my infamous concert that resulted in the deaths and injuries of several spectators. Sold out. Over sold, actually. Thousands of fans jammed together. There was a scene, a skirmish, some riled up guys and someone trying to storm the stage. Security intervened and... The timing was... We used pyrotechnics to enhance the show and... There was an explosion and screams and panic..." Her voice cracked. "My guitarist whisked me off stage. I never saw it. The chaos. The stampede for the exits. I learned about the casualties after."

"Dakota—"

"No. Let me get this out. There's something the public doesn't know. Something I need you to know."

She squeezed her hands together in a white-knuckled grip as if holding it together. "Two dead. Thirty-four injured. Some critically. I couldn't believe it. I didn't want to believe it. And on top of the tragedy came the awful accusations. Pointing the finger at me for whipping the audience into a frenzy. Faulting my team for overfilling the hall and for cutting corners by investing in unreliable special effects."

Wyatt listened with a heavy heart. His mom and stepfather had made those same accusations. The media had ripped Dakota and her production team to shreds. And Wyatt had swallowed every damning morsel because that had been his little sister lying in the hospital. His little sister who'd suffered multiple operations and physical therapy only never to fully recover.

"I wanted to reach out to every victim," she said. "To every family. I wanted to express my sympathy and regrets. To offer comfort and some sort of financial help, but it became this huge legal mess. Roger forbade me from personally interacting with any of the afflicted parties. I had all of these people—lawyers, friends—acting in my best interest, advising me to lay low. They sent me away to an island, released a statement to the media saying I was devastated by the tragedy and recuperating in private. Which was only partly true. I was devastated, but I didn't want to disappear. I wanted to help. Only Roger and his lawyers scared the crap out of me. So I stuck my head in the sand and I drank myself into oblivion to cope."

"That," she plowed on, "was the beginning of my downward spiral. Much of the last twelve years is a blur. But I've been getting it together. Unbeknownst to Roger, two years ago I started tracking a few of the people injured at the concert. I didn't make personal contact, but I tried to make a positive difference in their lives, mostly by gifting them with something they really needed—like a car or paying off a loan or..."

She flushed and looked away. "I guess that's part of the reason my finances are hurting, although considering I was worth millions, I guess I never expected the well to run dry so soon. Another reason why I'm determined to nail this comeback. The additional income will allow me to make additional restitution."

Wyatt's chest ached with massive regret. He'd not only misjudged her, he'd crucified her. He'd needed someone to blame for Kerry's plight and, aside from himself, Dakota had been an easy target. "I'm surprised someone didn't leak your good will efforts to the media."

"All the gifts were made anonymously. No one knows but Maggie. And you. I just... I want you to know I'm not a shallow screw-up. I mess up. A lot. But I'm getting a handle on that too. After this tour, I'm retiring for good and... I don't know what I'll do for sure, but I'll be saying goodbye to Dakota Breeze. Maybe by that time.... Maybe things won't be so complicated. For you or me." She looked at him with her heart in her eyes. "Maybe then there could be an us."

He dragged a hand down his face.

"Or, not. I'm sorry, Wyatt. I thought I could handle this. The sex. I thought if we indulged, maybe some of the fascination would fade. Instead, I'm more hung up on you than ever. I know you feel something, too. That's why I told you everything. The worst of me and the best of me. Even though the timing's not right now—"

"It's not the timing, honey, as much as the situation. I can get past it, I think, but I'm not sure you can. Especially now that I know how you tick."

She hugged herself, bracing. "What is it?"

"My sister, Kerry. She was one of the thirty-four injured at that Philadelphia concert."

Dakota blinked. "I... No. That can't be right. I know every name. No MacDermott."

"Kerry's my half-sister. Last name Perkins."

Her face blanched. "Kerry Perkins. Age fourteen. Trampled in the chaos. Spinal injury that resulted in paralysis."

Wyatt flashed on something Luther had said, something about Dakota never forgetting. She not only remembered his sister by name, she knew how Kerry had fared after the incident.

"*I know every name.*"

Her soul had been burdened with the suffering of thirty-six victims and even after twelve years, she'd yet to let go.

"She used to play the piano," Dakota said, her voice growing brittle.

"She still plays piano. She's twenty-six now. Teaches creative arts."

"She had dreams of attending Julliard. Of being a concert pianist."

"That was my stepfather's dream. Kerry wanted to play in a rock band. She wanted to tour with performers like you." Wyatt narrowed his eyes. "How did you know about Julliard?"

She bolted to her feet and paced. "Kerry was one of the kids I tried to reach out to before Roger and the lawyers shut me down and shuttled me off to the tropics. But her father intervened. He said I ruined his daughter's life. That she'd never walk again. He threatened legal action should I ever attempt to contact her again. I buckled just like I always buckle. He was so intimidating. So cruel. So—"

"I know. I've been knocking heads with Michael Perkins a good portion of my life."

Dakota whirled, wide-eyed and angry. "Why didn't you tell me about Kerry last night? Or this morning? Does Rusty know?"

Wyatt stood. "No. I've never discussed my family with Rusty. The fact that she asked me to come here, for you, that's just a bizarre coincidence."

"But why did you accept? How could you be okay with protecting the very person who hurt your sister?"

"It wasn't your fault."

"Are you saying you never blamed me?"

"I won't lie."

"Is this some sort of cruel payback then? Seduce me then break me?"

Crushed by the first teardrop, Wyatt pulled her into his arms. "I didn't mean for this to happen, Dakota. I never thought...You took me by surprise. This took me by surprise."

She choked back a sob. "You should have told Rusty no. You should have told me no when I invited you into this room. Complicated my ass, this is hopeless. Your sister was trampled at my concert and now she's bound to a wheel chair for life. How can you look at me and not think of that? How can I look at you and not be reminded?" She thumped a fist to his shoulder. "Damn you, MacDermott."

He tightened his hold, stroked her back. "For what it's worth, Kerry never blamed you. She always worshiped you. Still does."

"That only makes it worse." Dakota pushed out of his arms and wiped away tears with a noisy sniff.

"What are you doing?" he asked when she snagged her phone from her purse.

"Searching the net for a shuttle service. I can't stay here," she said with a quick glance toward the rumpled bed.

The bed where he'd brought her to orgasm twice before giving in to his own pleasure. His heart ached with the memory of them coming together. The wonder in her eyes. The taste of her lips.

"I want to go back to Kramer," she said, "but I don't want to inconvenience Luther after giving him the day off."

Selfless, even in her misery.

"I'll take care of it," Wyatt said while nabbing his own phone.

She swiped at more tears while hurriedly dressing—panties, bra, cheery sundress, which didn't seem so cheery anymore. She massaged her chest while struggling to strap on her sandals.

He sensed the pressure building and pushing at her from all sides, sensed her taxed emotions and sporadic thinking. She was ready to bolt, oblivious to her surroundings and safety. She needed to fly and that worried him because it meant she wasn't thinking straight. He watched her back now but what about in the future?

He dressed while booking the shuttle, ending the call just as Dakota threw her bag over her shoulder and sailed for the door. He gently nabbed her elbow and pulled her against him. He stroked her hair. "Breathe."

Wilting against him, she grabbed two fists of his shirt and clung. "Remember our agreement," she said, trembling with emotion. "What happened in this room stays in this room. When we walk out that door you're my bodyguard. Period. And only until I wrap things at Starstruck. I don't want to upset Rusty otherwise I'd send you packing tonight, MacDermott."

He allowed her to believe she had that power rather than escalate her upset. He wasn't going anywhere until he knew for certain no threat existed from that damn threatening letter.

She rose on her toes and brushed her mouth over his. He'd never known there was such a thing as a sad kiss.

"I hate you for making me love you," she said, shredding his heart as she walked out the door.

Eleven

Starstruck
Tuesday, June 16, the calm before the storm

"I don't know what happened," Van said as he approached the stage, "but you're like a new person this week, Dakota. Or should I say you're finally back to your old self."

"No," Brock countered. "She's better than her old self. There's a genuine fire to her performance that wasn't there before. And a maturity to her voice." The brutally honest choreographer pushed out of his director's chair and afforded Dakota a rare smile. "You impressed me during yesterday's rehearsal, but today... You dazzled, sweetheart. Nicely done."

The six dancers, who'd nailed the routines long before Dakota, circled around her now voicing enthusiastic praise. It meant a lot because A) They were all super talented, and B) She knew their compliments and support were genuine. That said, their praise didn't trump her own sense of accomplishment. At long last her self-worth didn't hinge on the opinions of others.

Winded and sweaty from two hours of intense rehearsal, Dakota toweled her face and swigged water while leaving the stage to join Van and Brock on the floor. Yes, she was exhausted, but she couldn't stop smiling. Nailing the complicated and physically demanding dances hadn't been easy. It had been even harder to power through the songs vocally without sliding off key or running out of breath. But she'd done it.

Reconnecting with her passion had helped.

Focusing on her ultimate goals had helped.

Knowing Mac had been lurking in the shadows—watching, listening—definitely helped. She hated to admit it, and she wouldn't out loud, but his presence was a fierce motivator. She needed to prove to herself that he hadn't crushed her beyond repair. That she hadn't lost sight of herself or her goals.

What's more, she needed to prove to him that she was fine, better than fine, and that she wouldn't fall apart when he moved on. As frustrated and hurt as she was by their impossible situation, she knew he was struggling, too. Even though he'd shifted back into Ice Man, Dakota now saw his cold indifference for what it was.

His secret weapon.

She copped attitudes, pulling the diva routine in order to brazen her way through emotional situations, to deflect potential hurt.

He shut down, closed himself off. Only now there was a crack in his armor and Dakota could see through it. She could see a glimpse of his heart and it was aching. He loved her. As crazy as it was, Wyatt MacDermott had fallen as quickly and deeply as Dakota.

If only she could be happy about that.

"Just so you know," Van said as she closed in, "I videoed that second-to-last segment and emailed it to Roger. Last week's progress reports made him twitchy, so I figured I'd give the old guy a boost. He texted me back. Wants to do a conference call with you, me, and Brock in five minutes. Let's take a seat."

Brock dismissed the dancers and the audio tech Rusty had scheduled to handle their rehearsals.

Van ushered Dakota across the massive dance floor.

During the day, an air wall separated the performance end of Starstruck from the main bar and dining area. Even though a lunch crowd buzzed on the other side of the wall, this side was quiet and isolated except for Dakota's immediate crew. As far as she knew Rusty was in her office and Mac, well, he was around. Somewhere.

"Where's Pauley?" she asked. His absence was unusual and hinted at trouble. The inclusion of another bodyguard had caused him to step up his game. The past two days he'd spent less time flirting with the dancers and more time flexing for the competition.

Just as Rusty had feared, a faction of the paparazzi had finally showed, buzzing around Dakota's temporary digs in addition to Starstruck and being a general pain for all concerned. At some point, and to everyone's surprise, Mac and Pauley had joined forces to keep intrusive photographers and reporters at bay.

"Some joker snuck in with a camera during your last number," Van said. "Pauley and your shadow escorted him outside. I'm not fond of MacDermott," he said while pulling a chair out for Dakota, "and I still don't understand why you agreed to Rusty's paranoid security decree, but I have to admit he's good at his job. Is he signing on for the full tour?"

"What? No. Why would you ask that?"

Van shrugged. "He's awfully protective of you."

"That's his job."

"Thought I sensed something more. I just... I'd hate for you to get distracted with so much at stake. And now that you're finally in the zone—"

"You don't need to tell me what's at stake," Dakota said, refusing to fall into old ways. "I know what's at stake, Van. Better than anyone. I don't need you or Roger or my dad to monitor and manipulate my actions. You were right. I'm a new person. And this person can think and choose responsibly for herself."

Van raised two hands in defense just as his phone rang.

Brock settled in and Van put Roger on speaker for the three way conference.

Dakota sat rigid in her seat listening to her mentor gushing about her taped performance. He complimented Brock and heaped praise on Van. He said all the right things to Dakota and enough of the wrong things to keep her on edge. When he segued into an obvious ploy to guilt her into staying the course, she clenched her jaw, biting back a dose of what she'd just given Van. Now wasn't the time.

"I knew you'd bounce back, sweetheart. I just didn't expect it to happen so fast. And from what I saw in that short video," Roger said, "you're stronger than ever."

"You sound surprised," Dakota said, angry at herself for feeling a little hurt.

"You've been out of the game a long time. And there's your sketchy history. I've had a hard time convincing promoters and buyers that, after all this time and all that's happened, you can fill their venues. This video will help. I'll be passing it on to my contacts and leaking it to social networks. With any luck it will go viral. Let's get some positive buzz going, folks."

"Pro-active," Van said. "I like it."

"What Van caught on vid," Brock said, "is some of my best work and some of Dakota's finest dancing. Going viral is a given."

Dakota wasn't sure how she felt about this, not that anyone asked.

"Speaking of press," Roger plowed on, "Van mentioned that the pap showed."

"Security is keeping them at bay," Dakota said.

"Yeah, well, let's loosen up on that."

"What do you mean?"

"Van also told me about Open Mic night at Starstruck. Every Wednesday, right? Let's take advantage," Roger said.

Dakota blinked. A chance to repeat the magic she'd experienced in secret on Sunday? Only this time in front of the audience? "You want me to sing with the band?" she asked. "To surprise everyone by sitting in on some cover tune?"

"God, no," Roger said, sounding horrified. "We'll arrange for you to be featured. A surprise appearance, yes, but a planned performance to tracks. A taste of what I saw from today and what they can expect at future concerts. Talk to Rusty, Van. Make it happen. And tell her muscle to back off tomorrow night. I want the paparazzi there. Advance press. Positive press. Are you with me, Dakota? I need you to rock the house. There's a lot at stake, babe."

Van shot her a look.

Dakota clenched her fists in her lap. "I'll rock it."

She had her own reasons for wanting positive buzz. She was focused on a comeback tour, on repairing her tattered reputation, and replenishing finances. She was determined to continue her anonymous efforts to brighten the lives of those who'd suffered via the fallout of her infamous concert. She was specifically determined to make a positive difference in the life of a young woman who humbled Dakota with her resilience and misplaced worship.

Even though Mac would soon be out of the picture, Kerry Perkins was very much on Dakota's radar.

* * *

"I don't like it."

"What's not to like MacDermott?" Van Mitchell regarded Wyatt as though he were a petulant child. "It's a win-win. Dakota performs for a packed house. The crowd goes bonkers and bombards social media with photos and videos. Couple that with the powerhouse coverage of the paparazzi which will lead to interest from mainstream media. Free publicity, man. Positive publicity. Dakota will benefit. Starstruck will benefit."

Unless Dakota choked on stage. She'd almost frozen on Sunday and the only pressure had come from herself. How would she fare in front of a live audience? What if there were hecklers? What if she buckled under pressure? And that was just one of Wyatt's concerns.

Kyle Burns had yet to match prints from that letter to a person of interest. Wyatt had no leads on the identity of a nutjob who might mean Dakota harm. Putting her up on that stage was as good as putting a bull's-eye on her forehead. Unfortunately, he couldn't voice that concern since Dakota still refused to "needlessly" worry her team. Burn's failure to confirm the threat, combined with the fact that there had been no additional threats, had instilled her with a false sense of security.

"Too risky," Wyatt said then glanced at Rusty for backup.

Seated behind her desk, the fireball owner of Starstruck glanced from Wyatt to Dakota then back to Van Mitchell. "Dakota's my friend. Naturally, I want to support her. But my first responsibility is to this club. The patrons and my employees. I'm worried about crowd control. You're right. Wednesday nights are packed. Dakota's certain to cause a stir. If things get out of hand..."

Dakota flinched and Wyatt knew she was thinking about Philadelphia. "I'll tone it down," she said.

"What?" Van's eyes bugged. "Absolutely not! Toning down your performance defeats the purpose."

"One number," Dakota said to Rusty. "I'll be on and off in no time."

"I'm not only concerned about safety in the house," Rusty said with a pointed look at Dakota. "I'm worried about the performers on stage. I'm worried about you."

"What do you think, people are going to lob corn nuts at her head?" Van blasted. "Did you see Dakota in rehearsal today? They're going to love her!"

Wyatt was two seconds from dragging the man into the hall for a dose of reality. Yes, the majority of the audience would love her, but there was at least one person out there who wanted her to crawl back in her hole.

"I'll be under the watchful eyes of Pauley and MacDermott," Dakota said. "I'll be fine."

She glanced over at Wyatt then, finally, and his heart jackhammered in his chest.

"If at any time during the performance you tell me to bail," she went on, "I'll bail. Unflinching trust."

"I hate you for making me love you."

She was killing him.

"There you have it," Van said. "Everyone happy now? Great." He pressed his phone to his ear. "On for tomorrow, Roger. Let's do this and do it big." He disconnected then looked at Dakota. "You," he said, "are taking the rest of the day off. But first, let me take you to lunch. I found this place in town that makes great salads."

"I'd rather have a cheeseburger," she said causing Wyatt to smile a little as Van hustled her out the door. Unfortunately, she didn't give Wyatt a second look.

"I don't like it," Rusty said in their wake.

"That makes two of us," Wyatt said as he shifted to follow. "Do you think Charlie can call in a few friends? Beef up security for tomorrow night."

"I was talking about whatever went wrong between you

and Dakota. You two have been keeping your distance ever since you returned from Chicago and neither one of you have seen fit to confide in me, even though I've been none too subtle about offering a sympathetic shoulder. A little insulting since I consider you both friends. Be that as it may, whatever caused this riff, I don't like it. I don't like that my friends are hurting."

"That makes two of us," Wyatt muttered again as he blew past Rusty's well-meaning lecture in order to protect the woman he'd loved and lost in the span of forty-eight hours. The freaking clusterfuck of his life.

And Rusty wondered why he didn't want to talk about it.

Twelve

Wednesday, June 17, the night of reckoning

The day passed in a blur. Just like the day before and the day before that.

Somehow Dakota managed to make it through the morning and afternoon without ever being alone with Mac. The tension between them was excruciating. He was every bit the distraction Van feared him to be and Dakota unraveled a bit every time she chanced his gaze.

Her temporary bodyguard. Her fleeting lover. Her eternal inspiration.

Their enigmatic bond fueled her passion every bit as much as her secret performance with Bathwater Funk. Even though her emotions were tangled, her spirit had never been freer. She'd spent the last three nights falling to sleep while spinning scenarios. Positive scenarios.

It helped that Burns hadn't tied that venomous letter to an ominous source. It helped that there had been no additional threats. She couldn't help thinking that she'd been right to pass the letter off as a mean-spirited but harmless prank.

Wishful thinking if you asked Mac.

That was another reason she'd kept him at bay throughout the day. He'd made it clear that he was against tonight's performance. He anticipated trouble. He expected her to stoke the crowd into a dangerous frenzy. And she assumed he couldn't help but worry that someone in the audience would get hurt. The way his sister had been hurt. That thought speared Dakota's heart over and over and doubled her fear that she would forever remind him of Kerry's darkest day.

"I don't know how you apply those false lashes so flawlessly," Maggie said, looking over Dakota's shoulder and admiring her efforts in the mirror.

"Lots of practice." Dakota turned away from the vanity and provided her assistant with a full-on look. "I'll apply more blush and lipstick after we get to the club, but what do you think?"

Maggie pushed her tortoise shell glasses higher on her nose. "You look glamorous. Your hair. Your makeup."

"What about my costume?"

"Oh. Well, it's, um, daring?"

Dakota raised a brow. "Is that your nice way of saying trashy?"

Maggie blanched. "No. Of course not. I'd never—"

"Relax." Dakota sighed then pivoted toward the antique full-length mirror in the corner of her room. "It is sort of trashy," she said noting the way the black leather bodysuit hugged her every curve. "I'm surprised Brock didn't work a whip into the sequence. But at least it's not a studded bikini. It could have been worse."

"Why do you have to wear a costume at all?" Maggie asked. "It's Open Mic night. Everyone else who sits in will be in normal clothes. You'll stand out."

"That's the idea."

"But wouldn't you rather be applauded for your talent than your body?"

"You know I would." Dakota had lamented that sentiment to her gentle assistant more than once over the past year.

"Then why—"

"Because it's part of the package we're selling," Dakota snapped. "Sorry," she added in a softer tone. "I'm wound a little tight."

Summoning calm, she pulled on an ankle-length duster. A shimmering silver number that she was supposed to tear off on the first chorus of *I'm a Wild Child*. Her selected number for tonight was a new song on her roster and not an old hit. At least the audience, and the million people who viewed any captured moments on the Net, wouldn't compare this performance with one from a decade ago.

"Did you return your dad's call?" Maggie asked as Dakota tossed her monster cosmetic bag into a monster tote alongside mega-hold hair spray and assorted other necessities.

"I did." The little girl in her had been anxious to hear his praise. Unfortunately, even thought he'd voiced pride regarding her recorded rehearsal, their strained relationship diluted her pleasure. They hadn't been on good terms for a long time, so his enthusiastic well wishes for tonight had felt awkward at best. All in all, a disappointing conversation.

"And he thinks leaking tonight's performance to social media is a good thing?" Maggie asked.

"He does." And from a marketing standpoint, so did Dakota. At least they weren't at odds on *everything*. "Is there something on your mind, Maggie?"

The woman worked the hem of her retro-forties blouse. Although she'd recovered from that horrible virus, her mood was still somber. "It's just that you made tremendous progress over the last year. You seemed happier. And you were making a positive difference, well, you know. I hate to see you getting dragged back into..."

Dakota met her troubled gaze. "Into what?"

"Nothing. It's just, it's such a fickle and toxic business."

"True. But it's not all bad." And this time around Dakota was determined to use the rewards for good. She texted Mac that she was ready to leave then looked back to Maggie who was gathering Dakota's tote and purse.

"You should come tonight," Dakota said. "It'll do you good to get out. Have a few drinks. Enjoy the show. Not just me, but the band, Bathwater Funk. They're fabulous and—"

"I don't like crowds."

"I know," Dakota said, her heart swelling for her socially awkward friend. "But you need to get used to them. When we go on tour—"

"Things will be different. I know." She smiled a little. "I'll come."

"Great. I'll take all the support I can get." She hugged Maggie then rolled back her shoulders and practiced her most dazzling smile. "Let's roll."

* * *

Wyatt was waiting in the hall when Dakota stepped out of her room looking outrageously gorgeous.

"Maggie's coming with us."

One more person to protect. Wyatt held Dakota's gaze. "You sure about that?"

Dakota faltered for a second then glanced at her bookish assistant—a wisp of a thing whose glasses looked too big for her face and whose vintage get-up looked vastly out of step with Dakota's hip sophistication. Yet Dakota regarded her with easy acceptance and affection.

"Stick close to Pauley," she said.

"Pauley will be busy looking out for you," Wyatt said while reaching to relieve Maggie of Dakota's bags.

"I have them," Maggie said, holding tight. "Thanks anyway."

"You'll be on the job, too, MacDermott," Dakota said. "I'm not worried."

That made one of them.

"I can stay behind," Maggie said.

"Don't be silly," Dakota said. "Nothing bad is going to happen. MacDermott's overly cautious. Goes with his job." She nudged Maggie forward then turned and whispered at him. "Stop trying to scare my assistant."

"I'm trying to scare you."

"I can't hide forever."

"I'm not asking you to hide. I'm asking you to exercise caution."

"I'm not going to do anything irresponsible, if that's what you're afraid of. I'm going to deliver a solid performance. Period. If I'm lucky the crowd will react favorably with enthusiastic applause, but it's not like they'll go ape-shit when I hit the stage. You're forgetting I'm not a big deal anymore."

"You're a big deal to me."

She swallowed then blushed. "That wasn't a very

professional thing to say."

"I know." But he wouldn't take it back. "I've spent most of my adult life locking down my emotions, Dakota. It seemed like the smart thing to do considering they bit me in the ass when I was younger. I spoke up and acted out—once with my stepfather, once in the military. Both instances ended badly. Then I learned about my sister's accident. I lost it. With the doctors. With my family. I was angry and heartsick and ripped up with guilt."

"Guilt?"

"If I hadn't joined the military to escape my controlling stepfather, I might have been there to help when Kerry rebelled. She looked up to me. She trusted me. Instead of sneaking off to your concert, she might've invited me along. If I'd been there..."

"Maybe you could have prevented her from being trampled?" Dakota frowned. "You could have just as easily been injured or killed yourself, Wyatt."

"That's what Kerry said."

"I'm sure she never blamed you for her misfortune."

"She never blamed anyone. That's part of Kerry's beauty. She rolled with the punches and reinvented her life. I admire the hell out of her." His heart kicked. "I admire you."

He cupped Dakota's stymied, glammed-up face, reflecting on the beauty within. "I never told you how much your performance affected me on Sunday. You moved me, Lucy Shaw. Deeply. Your performance. Your voice. Magic."

Tears shimmered in her eyes. "Why are you telling me this now?"

"Because you're determined to go through with this performance and that means I'll be busy watching your back. This might be our only private moment and I want you to hit that stage knowing I'll be going ape-shit over you. On the inside, of course."

"Of course." She laughed a little and blinked back tears. "You kind of suck for going sappy on me right after I applied my makeup."

"Yeah, well." He wanted to kiss her. God, how he wanted to kiss her.

His phone rang. He glanced at the screen then answered. "What's up, Pauley?"

"Yo, Mac. Luther's here. The buzzards on the other side of the gate snapped a ton of photos when he drove through and they just snapped several more when I ushered Mr. Mitchell and Maggie into the sedan. You might want to warn Dakota."

"I'll let her know." He pocketed his phone and readjusted his holster.

"Show's on?" Dakota asked with a brave smile.

Heart pounding, he gave her hand a reassuring squeeze then took the lead. "Show's on."

* * *

They arrived at Starstruck just after ten. A small league of photographers had followed the sedan from the house to the club. According to Mac who got a call from Rusty, most of the paparazzi were already inside along with numerous music lovers. Dakota's dancers had arrived early as well and were backstage warming up. The parking lot was overflowing and a crowd of people were still waiting to get inside.

Dakota's pulse raced as Luther dropped Van, Maggie, and Pauley in front—a decoy of sorts—then zipped around to the back of the club.

Her senses went haywire as Mac rushed her inside and through the back halls. She'd been rushed into hundreds of venues. She'd performed for hundreds of thousands of people. This was nothing. This was a moderately-sized club in a tiny Midwestern town. One song. That's all she had to get through. Not a whole show, not even a full set. Yet the anticipation was close to paralyzing.

"Just do this," she whispered to herself. "Get it over and get on with the future."

Suddenly she couldn't hear her own thoughts let alone her whisper or anything Mac was saying. The music was blasting and a guest singer was mangling the melody of *Freebird*. Dakota smiled to herself, remembering how Rusty had mentioned Bathwater Funk was always fielding requests for classic favorites time and again. Even though the singer's voice wasn't pitch perfect, the man had heart. Emmett was wailing on slide guitar and Quinn was laying down a groove that reinforced Dakota's love of live music.

Minutes later she was alone in a small dressing room with

Rusty. The dancers were dressed and waiting backstage. Maggie was in the wings with Pauley. Van was front of the house and Mac was doing whatever he did when he was in full protector mode.

"I can't remember the last time I was this nervous," Dakota said as Rusty rigged her with a pocket transmitter and headset condenser mic. "It's kind of a good feeling, if that makes sense."

"Means you're connected," Rusty said. "Means you care. Means you'll knock them dead, honey." She tweaked the wireless rig that allowed Dakota to dance and sing sans a handheld mic. "You're all set. Dwight will unmute your channel when you hit the stage. He already has your track cued up and ready to go. I'll tell the band to break after one more song. After that, I'll take over as host and announce you as a surprise special guest. Even though it's not much of a surprise. Word got out and most of these people are here to see you, honey."

"They're probably expecting a train wreck."

"Well, now won't they be disappointed?" Rusty winked then scooted out.

Stomach fluttering, Dakota opened her tote in search of her cosmetics and hairspray. Five minutes to show time. "I can do this."

Her bravado plummeted when she saw an envelope. Right there in her bag. On top of her beauty supplies. She noted her name glued to the front in a montage of cut-out letters.

DAKOTA

Trembling, she opened it without thinking, desperate to know the content. The letter featured a collage-like message, similar to the first anonymous letter only the wording was different.

"Continue down this wicked path," she read aloud, "and you'll live to regret it."

The letter fluttered from her hands as she stumbled back, stunned.

Mac appeared in the doorway. "Dakota, I..." He took one look at her face. "What is it?" He moved inside as she stooped for the letter. He took it from her and read.

"I don't understand, Wyatt. The first letter threatened to

kill me. This says I'll live to regret it. Conflicting messages."

"Where did you find it?"

"In my bag."

"The bag Maggie carried in."

"Any one could have slipped the letter inside as she and Van made their way through the crowd. Also, she left it here in the dressing room for me. I'm sure she thought it was a secure area. But maybe someone snuck in or was waiting or... I don't know. I..." She faltered as the music ended and Rusty's voice rang over the mic. "I have to go. That's my cue."

"You're not going on."

"The hell I'm not. Flake out on another engagement? With the paparazzi out front and primed to report to the public? There's too much at stake."

"Nothing is as important as your safety."

Rusty's enthusiastic patter revved Dakota's impatience. She glanced toward the stage.

"I say bail, you bail," Mac said. "Remember?"

"I'm sorry, Wyatt." The professional in her wouldn't allow her to miss her cue. And the part of her that wanted so badly to make things right wouldn't give in to fear. She bolted into the wings as Rusty segued into a sentimental and funny story about the first time she met Dakota behind the scenes of an award show.

Mac caught Dakota by the arm. "The messages aren't conflicting. Think about it. *Crawl back into your hole or suffer my wrath. Continue down this wicked path and you'll live to regret it.* We were wrong about the first taunt. Not a blatant death threat directed at you."

"Suffer my wrath," she said. "You'll live to regret it."

Regret.

Regret.

She peered beyond the wings, homing in on the people crushing right up to the edge of the stage. What if they were the ones at risk? Or her dancers? What if someone was somehow threatening a replay of the Philadelphia debacle? But who? And why? Dakota's mind scrambled as Rusty drew closer to calling her on stage. An epiphany hit her from out of nowhere and with the force of a freight train.

"Oh, my God. It's Maggie."

"What?"

"I think Maggie concocted those letters, Wyatt. I don't think she'll make good on the implied threats, but I can't be sure."

He didn't ask why or how. He touched his ear then spoke and Dakota realized he was also rigged, but with some sort of surveillance communication. "Pauley, is Maggie with you? Van? No?" He bit off a curse. "No, stay where you are and keep your eye on Dakota."

Rusty ended her story and the crowd applauded. "You know her. You love her," she said over the mania, "but not half as much as me. Please welcome to the Starstruck stage, Dakota Breeze!"

I'm a Wild Child blasted through the speakers. Eight bars to make a solo entrance then The Darlings would spiral in during the next eight. Dakota grabbed Wyatt and spoke close to his ear. "If Maggie does try something it will be down front, close to the stage where I can see it!" She kissed him then, swift and hard. "I trust you to keep me safe. To keep everyone safe."

And with that she strutted on stage with as much grace and courage as she could muster. She focused on the music, her voice, and her moves. She fed off her adrenaline and the audience's energy.

Blinded by the stage pars and two spotlights she couldn't see the bulk of the spectators, but she could clearly see the people on the dance floor, the two rows of music lovers crushed closest to stage. Pumping their fists, clapping their hands, grooving to the pounding, techno beat.

The Darlings surrounded her on an instrumental solo and together they broke into a complicated dance segment. Dakota imagined Brock smacking his hand to his forehead, thinking she'd forgotten to tear away her shimmering duster. She purposely skipped that part as it was intended to titillate and rile the men specifically.

Exercising caution, she thought to herself and she poured her heart into the next verse.

But then she heard a pop and saw a flash. A blur of commotion and confusion. People pushing, shoving. A thrown punch. She saw Charlie and Mac closing in. Saw Maggie struggling in the crush.

She caught Mac's eye and pointed, certain Maggie was in

harm's way. Even though she didn't miss a beat or note, Dakota flashed back on Philadelphia. She saw Pauley moving toward her, intent on whisking her off stage. She waved him away. She wouldn't leave. She wouldn't draw more attention to a fist fight or whatever it was. Her heart thudded as she pressed on, playing it cool even though she was out of sorts. She gave her all and then some. Demanding the attention of the crowd with a flashy performance as Mac whisked Maggie up and away and Charlie and his crew quickly dissipated the fray.

Open spaces quickly filled with more eager fans, all smiling up at Dakota, all grooving to the music. No panic. No commotion. No scrambling toward the exits.

She powered toward the end, the final dance sequence, the final note.

The audience exploded into deafening applause. Cameras flashed as several voices echoed, "Encore!"

Dakota's felt dizzy with relief and joy. But mostly confusion. For a heart-stopping moment, she'd relived her worst nightmare. And that moment had been instigated by a person she considered a friend. She wasn't sure how and was vague on the why, but the betrayal left her heartsick.

Rusty rushed on stage, allowing Dakota a graceful exit. The band kicked back in before she even made it backstage. She held it together as the dancers expressed their glee with a seamless performance while making mention of the spontaneous tussle.

Van whizzed in. "What tussle? What... God, that was great, Dakota! Look, look," he said while showing her his phone. "You already hit Twitter!"

"Why didn't you reveal your bodysuit," Brock asked. "Never mind. You'll get it next time." He shoved an iPad in her face. "Look at what's already posted to YouTube."

Mac pressed in, sans Maggie. "She's in Rusty's office with Pauley," he said to Dakota. "You were right and it's not pretty, but we'll sort it out. The question is whether or not to involve the police."

"What's this about the police?" Van asked, red-faced.

"If this is going to reflect bad on Dakota," Brock started.

She blew past both of them, flinging herself into Mac's arms. She cried. She couldn't help it. A hundred emotions battered her being. And under it all, one heartbreaking realization.

Now that she was safe, he'd be leaving.

Thirteen

"I can't believe it," Luther said. "I just can't believe it."

"Yes, well now that you know," Van said, "forget what you heard."

"I don't take orders from you," Luther said as he steered the car toward the estate.

Van looked over his shoulder, into the shadows of the darkened backseat. "Dakota."

"It would be best for everyone if we kept this under wraps, Luther. Maggie will have a hard enough time recovering from this mess without it becoming public."

"Maggie will have a hard time?" Van grunted. "She harasses you with anonymous letters—which you should have told me about before, by the way—tries to sabotage your performance—who sets off a frickin' firecracker in a crowded room?—and you're worried about *her*?"

Wyatt reached over and squeezed Dakota's hand. She squeezed back but instead of letting go, she held tight. His chest hurt, knowing she was clinging to their last night together. He wanted to cling, too.

"I still say you should press charges," Van said.

"I don't understand why she did it," Luther said.

"You may not believe it," Dakota said, "but she was looking out for what she thought was my best interest."

"You're right," Van said. "I don't believe it."

"She thought if I resurrected my old persona and returned to touring, I'd revert to my old, shallow ways," Dakota went on. "Destructive thinking, partying. Performing as Roger's puppet instead of following my own heart."

"Well, that's a crock," Van said.

"No, it's not," Dakota countered. "It's a valid concern, although I promise you none of that will happen. She was also worried I'd abandon a good will project we were working on. That won't happen either. In fact, it's the motivating factor in my conceding to this tour and the dictated performances."

"What project?" Van asked.

"It's private."

Wyatt absorbed everything Dakota said and didn't say. He respected her agenda. And even though he worried about how she'd fare with a team that seemed intent on manipulating her, he honestly believed she'd muscle through with her personal goals intact. What he couldn't imagine was joining her tour as her personal bodyguard. Something Van had suggested after their confrontation with Maggie. Something Dakota hadn't commented on. He knew her mind. It wouldn't work. Their relationship was personal now and there was no going back.

"At any rate," Dakota said, breaking the tense silence, "I feel sorry for Maggie. On top of everything she was convinced I'd replace her after we went on tour. She's not cut out for that life."

"She should have thought about that before she applied for a job with a celebrity," Van said. "Jesus. But whatever. Thankfully, we curbed her crazy behavior before it got worse. I still think we should have turned her over to the police, but apparently I'm not calling the shots."

"No," Dakota said, casting Wyatt a small smile. "That would be me."

"At least you agreed to put her up in a hotel overnight," Van said, "instead of allowing her to sleep under your same roof."

"I feel sorry for her," Dakota said. "That doesn't mean I trust her."

"Sad, but smart," Luther said as he pulled through the

gate and into the drive.

"Just hang here while I run inside and gather Maggie's belongings," Van said to Luther. "I'll need a lift back to the hotel. Not that I don't trust Pauley to keep an eye on Little-Miss-Psycho, but I'll feel better if I'm there. I'm personally putting Maggie on a plane tomorrow. I'll also arrange for our return to LA. I thought we'd need the rest of the week to get you up to speed, Dakota. But we don't. Another day and we're out of here. Meanwhile, I trust I'm leaving you in good hands tonight with MacDermott." Brow raised, he pointed at Wyatt. "You don't talk much, do you?"

Wyatt met Dakota's gaze, his heart in his eyes. "Only when I have something to say."

* * *

The walk to her room was the longest walk of Dakota's life. And not because Mac walked behind her in silence. She'd grown used to his silence. She sort of liked it now. There was calm in his quiet. A serene confidence that soothed her soul. A nice contrast to the creative passion that stoked her spirit.

"I'm going to miss you bossing me around," she said as they reached her door.

"You say that now," he said with a teasing glint in those striking grey eyes. "When I'm presently *not* bossing you."

She grasped the lapels of his ever-present suit jacket. Ever the professional. "Thank you for tonight."

"You're the one who targeted Maggie."

"That was luck. Some things she said tonight. Some things she said in the past. They all came together in that one frantic moment before I went on stage. It was a gut feeling."

"Never dismiss instincts, Dakota."

She swallowed past a lump in her throat. "I think I'd like it if you called me Lucy. I feel like myself when I'm with you."

"That's a hell of a compliment, Lucy."

Her heart thudded. Oh, how she wanted to kiss him. "I'm going to need a personal bodyguard, someone other than Pauley," she said. "Not that he didn't rise to the occasion these last couple of days, but he's not you."

"I—"

"I know it can't be you, but maybe someone from your agency?"

He nodded. "I'll make sure Ian assigns his best man."

She raised a brow. "Wouldn't that be you?"

He smiled. "His second best then."

"So... is this goodbye?"

"Not quite." He smoothed her hair from her face then traced his finger down the curve of her jaw. "That last kiss in Chicago, it was a sad kiss. Then tonight...that kiss was fleeting and frantic."

Pulse skipping, she moistened her lips. "Are you hoping for another kind of kiss?"

"I am."

"A kiss to remember me by? A kiss to take into your dreams?"

"Sweet dreams of you."

Her insides turned to mush. "You remembered the opening line of the song."

"I remember everything about that moment. That performance. My first glimpse of Lucy Shaw."

He kissed her, tangling his fingers in her hair and crushing his mouth to hers.

She clung and kissed him back. With all her heart. All her hope.

"The lyrics to that song," she said when they eased apart. "They're about a lost love. Don't think of us as lost, Wyatt. At some point...it won't be so complicated. Don't give up on us."

"Now who's bossing who?"

"Say it."

He kissed her again, a slow, deep kiss geared to haunt her every dream. "I won't give up."

Fourteen

Kramer, IL
Saturday, September 5, the dawn of forever

"This is amazing. I can't believe we're here and I can't believe I've got my own private deck for a double billing. Rusty Ann Baker *and* Dakota Breeze. Freaking Dakota Breeze! This is amazing!"

"So you've said about a hundred times in the last hour."

"You're exaggerating."

"Not much." Wyatt smiled over at his sister. Twenty-six-years-old and, even with all she'd been through, with the challenges she faced every day, she still had the enthusiasm of a teenager. Kerry possessed the same fire she'd had twelve years ago when she'd last seen Dakota on stage. Only this time, Wyatt was at her side.

Truth was he was grappling with his own version of awe and anticipation.

Three months had passed since he'd last been here at Starstruck. Three months since he'd kissed Lucy Shaw goodbye. They'd kept in touch while she was on tour, but only a brief text here and there. No lengthy discussions. No regrets. No promises. Just thoughtful assurances that she was okay and he was okay. He buried himself in work, but he didn't bury his emotions. Not entirely. Ian had keyed in on that change. So had Kerry. Although Wyatt had never shared the details of that whirlwind week with Dakota, they both suspected he'd lost his heart on the job. What he hadn't lost, was hope.

"Fantastic! You're here and settled in," came a familiar voice. "Charlie told me, but I had to see for myself."

Wyatt stood as Rusty rushed toward them.

Dressed in tight jeans and a spangled red top, she smiled at Kerry then moved straight into Wyatt's arms for a quick hug. "I'm so glad you're here."

"You called, I came."

"Frank's looking forward to meeting you after the show. And Dakota—"

"Thanks so much for inviting us, Miss Baker," Kerry piped in. "And for arranging this private viewing from the Star Deck."

"Best seats in the house and totally my pleasure," Rusty said as she turned her attention to Kerry. Instead of standing over his sister and her motorized wheel chair, the veteran country star dropped into the seat Wyatt had vacated. "After the show I'll bring the band up and we'll have a private party. By the way, call me Rusty. Everyone does and besides your brother and I have been friends for a long time. I'd like us to be friends as well."

Kerry beamed. "Wyatt's going to kill me for saying this, but *this* is amazing."

"With potential for awesomeness," Rusty said. "But I'll let Dakota explain that."

Kerry's eyes bugged. "She's coming up here?"

"Actually," Dakota said as she moved in out of the shadows. "You're coming downstairs. I hope."

Kerry swiveled her chair around and Wyatt struggled to keep his heart from beating out of his damned chest. He wasn't looking at Dakota Breeze as much as Lucy Shaw. Dressed in a gauzy patchwork ankle-length sundress with random sparkles on the flowing skirt, she personified a bohemian free spirit rather than a cutting edge pop star. Her smile lit up the whole damned balcony and warmed Wyatt to the bones.

She glanced at him with earth-rocking affection then

extended a hand to Kerry. "I hear you're a longtime fan, Kerry."

"You have no idea."

"I've been wanting to meet you for a long time. I—"

"I know," Kerry said, squeezing Dakota's hand with both of her own. "You don't have to go there."

Wyatt massaged his tight chest, watching as Dakota blinked back tears and his sister radiated with uncontainable excitement.

"Due to an extended summer session with some of my students, I wasn't able to make any of the stops on your comeback tour," Kerry said. "So this Labor Day show at Starstruck with you and Miss... with Rusty is an unexpected thrill."

"The thrill is mine," Dakota said. "Only one thing would make it better. As a longtime fan and, from all I've heard, a gifted musician, I was wondering if you might like to sit in for a few songs."

Kerry stared.

So did Wyatt.

"This will be my last performance as Dakota Breeze, so I want to go out in style. With my friend Rusty. And with you, Kerry. If you'll do me that honor. We can take the elevator down and you can get a feel for the baby grand. As you can see, it's right alongside Ray's keyboard set up. He can talk you through keys and chords if you're unfamiliar. There's also sheet music—"

"I know all of your songs," Kerry blurted. "And even if you perform something off the cuff, I've got a great ear."

"So you'll do it?" Dakota asked.

"Seriously? This is the chance of a lifetime! My kids won't believe it. *I* don't believe it!"

"Believe it," Rusty said with a smile then stood. "We don't have a lot of time before the doors open, so let's head down to the stage."

Kerry looked over her shoulder at Wyatt, mouthing, "Freaking amazing!" Then she tore after Rusty.

"You don't have to ask her twice," Wyatt said as Dakota fell in behind them. His emotions were all over the map and his heart was now on his sleeve.

Charlie met them at the elevator.

"Nice lanyard," Wyatt said, busting the ace security man's chops with a grin.

Charlie grinned back, passing Wyatt a matching lanyard, blue with hot pink guitars, only his badge said: *Guest*.

"This just gets better and better," Kerry said dragging her hands through her funky, choppy blue hair and admiring her own special pass, a badge that said: *Band*.

"We'll catch up," Wyatt said, pulling Dakota aside as the elevator doors closed on Rusty, Kerry, and smart-ass Charlie.

Alone now, he backed Dakota against the wall. So damned beautiful. Inside and out. "You could have given me a heads up."

She pressed her palms to his chest. "I wanted to surprise her. And you. I've been going over this in my head for weeks, Wyatt. You know about my good will mission. I kept at it and I managed to do something nice, to gift everyone with something significant, over the last three months. Everyone but Kerry. Nothing seemed special enough. A few weeks ago I remembered what you said about her dream. Wanting to tour with a rock band. I assumed a full tour was impossible given her dedication to that creative arts school and her students and, well, this seemed possible. Doable. And she'd be with you so she'd be safe."

His second chance and Dakota's redemption in one fell swoop. *Holy shit.*

"How did you know she would go for it?" he asked.

"I just knew. She's a rebel. She's a trooper. She's an artist."

He shook his head in wonder, smiled. "It's an incredible gift."

She moistened her lips. "I have to be honest. It's not just for Kerry. It's for you. And me.

You were right. She complicated things between us. There was my regret and your guilt. When you said you didn't blame me anymore, I believed you, but I worried I would forever remind you of Kerry's darkest day. This is my chance to change that view. Maybe after today, after you see her on stage living out her dream, maybe I'll remind you of her brightest day. Or one of them anyway."

Heart full to bursting, Wyatt dropped his forehead to hers.

"I met my financial goals, Wyatt. After today, I'm leaving Dakota Breeze behind and going back to my roots. My passion. I'm interested in musical theater. I'm also interested in encouraging kids to be true to themselves. Creatively, that is. I thought maybe Kerry could give me some pointers on that end. To be honest, I'm not sure about where I'm heading professionally, but personally—"

"Marry me."

She blinked. "What?"

"This is what happens when I don't lock down my emotions," Wyatt said. "I'm just hoping it won't bite me in the ass this time."

She laughed a little, a nervous laugh that gave him hope. "But—"

"Don't over think it and don't talk it to death," he said while brushing her mouth in a whisper soft kiss. "Just say, yes."

"Yes."

She kissed him stupid, wrapping her arms around his neck as he pulled her close, held her tight. By the time they eased apart, he was floating.

So this was a taste of what had turned tough-as-nails Ian into a sentimental softie.

Dakota smiled up at him as if knowing his mind. "I love you for making me love you, Wyatt MacDermott."

"I love you, Lucy Shaw."

She narrowed those gorgeous green eyes. "You kind of suck for making me all emotional before a performance."

"I'm sorry."

"No, you're not."

Smiling he pulled her into the elevator and against him for another kiss. "You're right. I'm not sorry. I'm in sappy-ass love."

MORE STARSTRUCK

Starstruck

WRECKED

CYNTHIA VALERO

A Secret Crush...

Talented songwriter, Sunny Burnett, shelves her dream of Nashville when her older sister is killed in a car wreck and helps her mother pick up the pieces of her shattered life. Two years later, her mother's still struggling and Sunny is desperate to help her. Dusting off her guitar, penning a new song, and marshaling her courage, she enters a duet contest, hoping to use the prize money to turn her mother's life around. She'll do anything to win. Even if it means partnering with the last man she should ask—her sister's ex-boyfriend, a gifted singer and Sunny's longtime secret crush.

A Clandestine Choice...

Curtis Bliss blames himself for Tuesday Burnett's death. And so does her family. Haunted by regret, he forfeits his musical dreams for years, until he's challenged by a most unexpected source—his ex's younger sister. Sunny Burnett blows him away by asking for his help and, in turn, offering him a tentative forgiveness. Even more surprising is the burning attraction that ignites and consumes them both.

Can the new lovers make their dreams come true after all? Or will the secrets they keep wreck them forever?

TEASER FROM WRECKED

"I'd give you anything else, Sunny. Anything in my power. I'd cut my heart out and hand it to you, what's left of it, if that's what you wanted. But I can't sing, and I especially can't sing on that stage."

"It's not for me. It'd take more than that for me to ask you for anything." She gripped her handbag again, almost like a lifeline. "It's for my mother."

Krista. His gut twisted tighter. Her house had been like a home for him. She'd been the mother he'd lost at fifteen. The last time he'd ever felt taken care of. The last time he'd eaten a home-cooked meal. And he'd appreciated her caring way more than she could ever know. He hadn't exactly paid her back in the way he'd planned.

"It's been a year and she's not getting better." Sunny smacked the hat again. "I need that prize money to start a cafe. I think it might bring her back to life. It has to."

His mouth worked, but he couldn't shove out any words.

"You want to give us something? You want to give us that last little piece of your heart? Give us this."

He almost asked when she'd grown so fierce, but he knew the answer. He also knew he couldn't say no, even as he wanted to run fast and far away.

"You're so grown up." The whisper slipped out.

"Tuesday's death didn't stop my bones from growing."

He noticed her long legs, her graceful neck, the gentle arch of her back. He noticed the way her hip jutted when she planted her hand on it. She reminded him of a warrior queen braced for battle. She was braced for him to say no. She was braced to launch another attack to change his mind, to remind him why he would indeed do her bidding.

And, to his absolute disbelief, his fingers left the hand truck and reached out to touch a lock of her hair.

It was as silky-soft as he remembered.

He curled it around his index finger, and she closed her eyes. Her chest rose and fell with sudden, labored breaths. He felt himself slipping under a strange, dangerous spell.

She smacked away his hand. Her eyes glinted again. "I'm not Tuesday."

"No, you're not," he said and her cheeks flushed red. "I'll sing on that stage with you just this once, Sunny. When you're contest is done, so am I."

Starstuck

JADED

ELLE J ROSSI

Marry me, Brooklyn...
Four years ago Brooklyn ran from that plea and straight toward what she dreamed would be a better future. An aspiring fashion designer destined for more than the boredom of small town life and the strain of a whiskey-saturated family, she launched herself toward the runways of New York.

I can't...
Emmett couldn't compete with the glitz of the big city, let alone erase Brookyn's emotional scars. When she turned down his proposal and left him behind, he poured what was left of his heart into his music. He got through with three rules: Play the guitar. Play the field. Forget about Brooklyn.

Now Brooklyn is back and the past and present collide inside Starstruck when Brooklyn fills in as lead singer for Emmett's band. Night after night of thumping bass and passionately sung lyrics reminds them of every delicious memory they ever shared. But a sizzling attraction can only go so far when emotions are raw and trust is fragile. Emmett still wants forever. Brooklyn is only good at temporary.

Can two hearts find a way to truly connect off the stage, or will they stay forever jaded?

* * *

TEASER FROM JADED

A strum of a guitar.

A voice.

One note.

Sustained.

The exhale to her inhale.

Years' worth of tension uncoiled. For a moment, just a blip of time really, Brooklyn could breathe again.

A new kind of tension tightened her muscles to the point she almost couldn't move. But she had to see what she already knew. She turned toward the stage as another note rang out, pure, strong, and sexy as hell.

Everyone else in the room faded away as her gaze took in one man and his guitar. He wasn't supposed to be here. She wasn't prepared for him. For these feelings.

Even if his song wasn't meant for her, the intimacy of the notes, his voice, melted her bones. God, those lips. She wanted to be the microphone. Wanted to feel his lips move across her mouth in a song as old as time. Her pulse hammered in rhythm with the strum of his guitar, quick, heavy.

Emmett Tyler.

In the flesh—in all his glorious flesh. He wore jeans and a dark t-shirt that hugged a torso cut from lean muscle. She zeroed in on the tattoo covering his right bicep. She wanted to trace the lines, to know the story, but from this distance she couldn't make out the design.

He looked like she remembered, only sexier, more mature, rugged, harder. So much harder. She searched his face and gasped when his eyes met hers. Something flashed in their depths. Brooklyn nearly chewed through her bottom lip.

She took a step forward before she caught herself. Emmett stopped playing and turned to walk backstage. The vortex that had sucked her in slammed closed, jarring her heart and her soul.

Brooklyn whirled around and swallowed the shot of vodka as if her life depended on it. Then she got up close and personal with Jenna. "You set me up." So many feelings were wreaking havoc on her system. Anger, betrayal, confusion...lust. And more. So much more. What the hell was she going to do?

Jenna had the nerve to smile sheepishly and offered Brooklyn her shot. "You'll thank me someday."

What could she say to that? She had no effing idea. So she said nothing, tipped her head back and let the alcohol sear her throat.

* * *

NOTE TO READERS

The only thing better than creating a new story world is creating a new world with artistic soulmates. Cynthia Valero and Elle J Rossi are two of my favorite writers. They are also my cherished friends and critique partners. Cynthia and I have also written books as a team and Elle is my sister (one of five!) The three of us have a long history and a great bond so brainstorming the concept behind STARSTRUCK was a pure labor of love. I hope you enjoyed OBSESSED and I hope you'll indulge in Cynthia and Elle's tales as well. If you enjoy our stories please consider writing a review on any e-tailer or review site (such as Goodreads). Spreading the word helps us to share the love. Your support is very much appreciated!

Visit my website to explore my many worlds. From steampunk to paranormal to contemporary. Something for everyone! www.bethciotta.com

ACKNOWLEDGMENTS

It takes several professionals to bring a book to life. Special thanks to EJR Digital Art for the fabulous cover art! My appreciation to my editorial team—Elle J Rossi, Cynthia Valero, Mary Stella, and Melissa Norr (Brazen Pen Editing). Much gratitude to digital formatter Amy Atwell (Author EMS) and my technical support, Steve Ciotta.

87245809R10071

Made in the USA
Lexington, KY
22 April 2018